Dark Fire

Angela Dorsey

Dark Fire

Original title: Horse Angel #1 – Dark Fire
Cover and inside illustration: Jennifer Bell
Cover layout: Stabenfeldt AS
Published by PonyClub, Stabenfeldt AS
Edited by Karen Pasacreta
Printing: GGP Media, Germany 2004

ISBN: 82-591-1143-8

Darkness. Where am I? The damp ground is beneath my fingers. It feels moist and fresh. I can sense energy rising from the earth like a mist, wrapping me in its embrace, restoring me.

I am always so weak after the Shifting, so blind and tired. But soon I will see. Soon I will move. I must be patient. Then I will find the evil that lurks here.

I can feel the one who called me, who is calling me still. He is so close. Jupiter... He is afraid for his girl. He knows there is something terribly wrong, but he cannot understand it, can not see what it is. He can only feel it. His fear has summoned me here.

But now I can see the stars, and the moon is hanging in the sky like a bright shiny penny. I am in a garden—an English country garden behind a beautiful old Manor house. And there to the side are the stables. I must go to Jupiter.

The first thing Lisa noticed as she walked across the pasture toward Evergreen Manor was that almost every light was turned on. Brightness spilled from the house, splashing from the unshuttered windows and spreading across the lawn at the front of the house in wide pools. As she crept closer to the fence bordering the lawns, Lisa crouched lower. She didn't want anyone to see her, especially Mr. Pickering's nephew, Jimmy. The last time Lisa had seen Jimmy, he had told her that Mr. Pickering wanted her to stop coming over to take care of the horses. Lisa didn't know whether to believe Jimmy or not. It didn't seem like the sort of thing Mr. Pickering would say. He had always been so kind to her.

Lisa slipped through the fence and approached the house, avoiding the bright patches of lawn. *I wish I could talk to Mr. Pickering,* she thought, and stopped for a moment to glance up at his bedroom window. His window was one of the few that were dark. *Maybe he's in one of the rooms downstairs. I need to ask him if what Jimmy said was right,* she decided. *Mr. Pickering asked me to take care of the horses when he first fell sick, and I don't know why he would change his mind. Maybe Jimmy told him that I wasn't doing a very good job, but it's not easy when I have to sneak away from home to take care of them. And I do a better job than Jimmy does. Half the time he forgets to give them fresh water, and he hardly ever remembers to give them grain.*

When Lisa reached the house, she bent down below the windowsill of the dining room. Cautiously she raised her head so she could see into the room. No one was there. Dirty dishes were strewn across the dining room table and some of the cupboard doors were wide open. Paintings hung crookedly on the walls. Though the cupboards were on the other side of the room, Lisa could see that the contents had been pulled out and left lying on the floor in disarray. She ducked down again and crept along the edge of the house.

Next, Lisa peered inside the small room her mom had used as a study before they sold Evergreen Manor. Mr. Pickering hadn't moved any of his own stuff into the room and the empty space with the cheerful yellow walls and tiny white fireplace made Lisa feel sad. When her mom had used the room it had always looked so warm and welcoming. Her mom's rosewood desk had sat facing the window, and two of the most comfortable chairs Lisa had ever curled up in had been in front of the fireplace. Now the room was completely empty. *Why would Mr. Pickering or Jimmy leave the light on in an empty room?* wondered Lisa. *Something strange is going on.*

When she reached the library, Lisa was just about to rise up to look in the window when she noticed a dark silhouette fall across the square of light on the lawn beside her. Someone was in the library, either standing near the window or looking out into the night. Lisa held her breath as she studied the shadow. The person looked too thin to be Mr. Pickering. When the shadow finally moved away, Lisa slowly stretched up on tiptoes to see into the room.

Jimmy was on the other side of the library with his back to her. Lisa watched in disbelief as he pulled a book from the bookshelf, turned it upside down, shook it, and then dropped it to the floor.

What on earth is he doing? she wondered. *Doesn't he know that most of the books are antiques?* She ached to yell, "Stop!" when he grabbed another book, shook it, and threw it on the floor. Yellowed pages fluttered across the rug. Lisa didn't know what to do. She knew the books were valuable and, besides, she *loved* books. She couldn't see how anyone could treat a book in such a careless, callous way. And what's more, she knew Mr. Pickering wouldn't allow it either. He loved books too. One of Lisa's favorite things to do was discuss the books she had read with Mr. Pickering because he knew so much about them.

Where is Mr. Pickering? Lisa wondered as she watched Jimmy throw volume after volume onto the floor. *Someone has to stop Jimmy before he destroys all the beautiful books.*

Where did the old man put it? There must be hundreds of these stupid books. It's going to take hours just to search the library. Dear Uncle wouldn't have to suffer so much if he would just tell me where it is. I'm going to find it eventually.

He wouldn't have told that brat where it is, would he? Maybe I shouldn't have gotten rid of her. I wonder if she'll tell me if I start being nice to her? No. She knows how I treat those nags. She'll never trust me now.

Maybe if I grab the kid, my Uncle will tell me what I want to know. He's stubborn, and nothing I've tried has made him give up so far...but if I threaten the kid, he might tell me. I think it's time to start playing rough.

What's her name again? Laura...Lisa? Something like that. What did he do with that address book of his?

Lisa sighed with relief as Jimmy seemed to tire of pulling the books off the shelves. He stepped over the heap of volumes and went over to the desk in the corner, then jerked out the drawers and dumped their contents on top of the desk. He began to rummage through the papers and office supplies.

What on earth is he doing now? Has he gone crazy?

Suddenly the door flung open. A gaunt old man stood framed in the doorway. *Finally,* thought Lisa. *Mr. Pickering is here. He'll stop Jimmy.* The men's voices were loud and angry. Lisa put her hands over her ears. She was so tired of hearing angry voices. *I won't be able to talk to Mr. Pickering tonight,* she realized. *He's too busy with Jimmy. Why can't Jimmy just go back to wherever he came from? Things weren't perfect before, but now they're even worse!*

Lisa turned and fled. The loud voices followed her until she ran around the side of the house and then, suddenly, she couldn't hear them anymore. She was surprised. *Could the house block the sound that well?* Lisa slowed her step and thought of turning back to see what had happened, but then changed her mind. *Mr. Pickering probably won the argument,* she decided with confidence. *And I have to go to the horses. Jimmy probably didn't feed them tonight. He was too busy wrecking the house. What a jerk!*

I can feel danger. The evil one is near. He is a predator with no conscience. Loud voices rise in the air: one full of hatred and only patience in the voice of the other. He is trying to use reason, trying to understand the angry one. Then silence. Abrupt silence. The patient one has been overtaken.

And I cannot intervene. This is something I learned long, long ago—to trust and obey the Great One. I have been sent here to help Jupiter and his girl, not to save this soft-hearted man who has been silenced. Though my heart cries with helplessness and sorrow at his pain, I know I must pass on.

Lisa hurried toward the stable. She hadn't been able to sneak away from home all day. It was Saturday. Her dad had spent the day at home and had the idea that they needed some family time together. *Great family time,* thought Lisa sarcastically. Her dad had been grumpy all morning and later that afternoon when Lisa's little sister, Molly, was pestering him, he got mad at her for hardly any reason at all. He even raised his hand as if he wanted to strike her. Both Lisa and Molly were frightened by his actions and their mom had been furious.

After the yelling died down, hours of tense silence filled the house. Finally, Lisa's dad had apologized to Molly. Molly forgave him instantly, and Lisa's mom softened toward him as well. Lisa still didn't know how they could forgive him so quickly. But most of all, she didn't understand why her father was so angry all the time anymore. She was just glad that the next day he had to go to the city for a week of business meetings.

Lisa knew her father was bitter about having to sell Evergreen Manor and most of their possessions. Her mom asked her once to try to be patient with him. She explained that he felt like a failure because he hadn't been able to make enough money to pay the debts they owed on their ancestral home. She said he felt like he had let them all down.

Lisa tried to look the other way whenever he did anything she thought was unfair. She tried hard to be understanding, but when her father found out she was going to Evergreen

13

Manor to help take care of the horses, Lisa lost patience. He had been angry with her for a long time, not even trying to understand her point of view. But, worst of all, he didn't care when she told him Jupiter was losing weight. He didn't care that Jupiter wouldn't eat unless she was there.

When Lisa told him Mr. Pickering was a nice man, he grabbed her by the arm, and marched her to her room. That was the first night she snuck out her window, and she had snuck out to Evergreen Manor every night since. She didn't even feel guilty about it anymore, especially after she found that his grip had left bruises on her arm. During the week that followed, Lisa wore long-sleeved shirts. She didn't want her mom to see the black and blue marks or, even worse, to have Mr. Pickering see them. Lisa knew he would only feel bad if he knew how much her father hated him.

Lisa slipped into the stable and pulled the door shut behind her before turning on the light. Quickly she walked toward the first stall, where a bright chestnut mare waited.

"I'm tired of all the secrets, Firefly, and all the bad feelings. I don't like sneaking around," she complained to the Thoroughbred mare. "Why can't people just get along with each other? Why can't they be more like horses?" She paused and twirled Firefly's forelock around her finger. "If I couldn't come here everyday, life would be too horrible. You and Jupiter, Topper and Dakota keep me from going crazy. You're the only normal ones in my life right now, especially since I can't talk to Mr. Pickering anymore."

Firefly nickered in reply and bobbed her blazed head.

"I missed you too," said Lisa and stroked the chestnut's face. Then she looked down at Firefly's hooves. "Your stall is filthy. What does Jimmy do all day besides mess up the house and tear things apart? It looks like he gave you some food and water at least."

Lisa stopped speaking when a loud, impatient neigh came from the other end of the stable.

"Jupiter, be quiet," said Lisa, hurrying to the farthest of the four occupied stalls. "I don't want Jimmy to know I'm here. You remember what he told me last time he saw me. He scares me." Lisa shivered, remembering her encounter with him.

Last week, she had walked into the stable and found Jimmy waiting for her, slumped against a bale of hay with a half full bottle of whiskey lying beside him.

"We won't be requiring your services any longer," he drawled. "In fact, if you come here again, I'll have you thrown out of here as a trespasser."

"Wha...what do you mean?" Lisa was so surprised she could hardly speak.

"I mean," said Jimmy, his voice growing louder as he climbed to his feet, "you don't live here anymore, and you're not welcome here anymore."

"But Mr. Pickering..." Lisa started to say.

"My uncle doesn't want you here anymore either," Jimmy yelled. "He's just too polite to tell you."

Lisa tried to talk reasonably to Jimmy for another minute or two, but when he yelled at her again and staggered toward her, she panicked and ran out of the stable.

Even now, she could hear his laughter burning into her ears. It had taken all her courage to go back later that night to feed and water the horses and clean their stalls. Since then, Lisa had avoided Jimmy but still managed to do all the things for the horses that he didn't do.

"Jimmy didn't give you anything to eat, Jupiter," said Lisa, opening the stall door and walking to the empty manger. She turned and threw her arms around his neck. The black gelding nuzzled her back. "You're so wonderful,"

Lisa said, her voice muffled by his mane. "What would I do without you to talk to? Everything is horrible at home. I even have to sneak around to see you. Why did Dad have to sell you and the other horses along with the house? I know we don't have enough money to board all four of you, but I miss you so much!"

There they are, Jupiter and his girl. They do not know I have slipped into the stable yet, though the others see me. It is easy to see the love and trust that Jupiter has for his girl. And that she has for him.

Firefly, how wonderful to meet you. Yes, your foal is doing very well. He is a dressage horse now. You need not worry about him. His person knows how wonderful he is too. He always looks for you when he goes out to the shows and someday you may see him again.

Topper, do not be nervous. Of course, I promise not to tell the others, but you should not feel badly. All beings do things they later regret. The only thing we can do is learn from our mistakes. And you must know that the man, whom you hurt, also hurt you. You were afraid and re-acted without thinking, and since then you have learned to stop and think before you act.

Hello Dakota. It is wonderful to meet you too. You are such a fiery young fellow. I know you miss your girl. I am sure she misses you too. How could she not?

Jupiter's girl finally sees me. She looks frightened. Why are humans always so hard to communicate with? They are so suspicious of their own kind. And sadly, I can understand why they do not trust one an-other. They can be so cruel, sometimes on purpose and sometimes with-out even knowing what they are doing.

Lisa felt a force like an electrical current coming from behind her, making the tiny hairs on the back of her neck stand on end. Wide-eyed, she turned around, frightened that she might see Jimmy behind her.

A girl was standing at Dakota's stall, stroking the Appaloosa pony's forehead with light fingertips. The girl looked to be about 17 or 18 years old and was tall and willowy. Waist length, golden hair cascaded down her back and seemed to shimmer and sway, though there was no breeze in the stable to brush against it. Lisa gasped as the girl turned to gaze at her with light hazel eyes. Her eyes were so pale and luminous that they appeared as golden as her hair.

The girl smiled at Lisa. "He misses his girl," she said.

"Who are you?" Lisa blurted out. "What are you doing here?"

"I am Angelica," said the girl.

"Why are you here in my, uh, Mr. Pickering's stable?" stammered Lisa, her voice unnaturally loud though she was trying to speak quietly. There was something different about this girl. Something strange. Lisa felt the electrical current brush around her again like an unseen, living creature.

"I wanted to see your horses," said Angelica. "I hope you do not mind. They are lovely, by the way. All four of them."

"They aren't mine anymore," said Lisa cautiously.

"You sold them?" asked Angelica, her expression puzzled. "But you love them. Why would you sell them if you love them?"

Angelica's voice was not accusing, only curious, but Lisa still felt defensive. "We didn't want to sell them," said Lisa. She was surprised at how angry she sounded and made an effort to speak more politely. "We *had* to sell them. My dad owed lots of money that he couldn't pay back, so he had to sell almost everything we had. We used to live here, at Evergreen Manor, and we loved it. We didn't want to go."

"I am sorry," said Angelica softly. "Was Jupiter your horse?"

"Yes, and I really miss him," said Lisa, reaching out to touch the black gelding's neck without turning away from Angelica. "Hey," she said suddenly. "How do you know his name?"

"It is written on the stall door," said Angelica. "And I think he looks like a Jupiter. Do you not think so, in all his midnight blackness and the single white spot on his forehead like the planet that shines into space?" She came closer to the black gelding and held her hand out to Jupiter. Lisa stepped back as Jupiter moved as close to Angelica as he could, leaning over his stall door. He put his head down and sniffed at her hand, then, when she stepped closer, he pressed his face against her body.

Lisa was surprised. While Jupiter wasn't afraid of anyone except Jimmy, she had never known him to be affectionate with strangers. She reached out to touch Jupiter's neck again as she watched Angelica lean forward and whisper into his ear. Lisa strained to hear what Angelica was saying but the words were as indefinable as the wind rustling the leaves in the trees. When Angelica fell silent, Jupiter nickered to her in response.

"What did you say to him?" asked Lisa.

"I just told him how much you miss him," answered Angelica. "But he already knows. He misses seeing you more often too. He told me he does not like the new man at the house, the younger one, but he likes the older man. He wonders why the older man has not come to visit him for many days."

"He really said that to you?" exclaimed Lisa. *Angelica must know Mr. Pickering and Jimmy*, she thought. *There's no other way to explain it. But how would she know that Jupiter didn't like Jimmy? And how could she know Mr. Pickering was sick and hadn't visited the horses for a while? This is too weird.* She pushed against Jupiter's chest and commanded, "Back." Reluctantly Jupiter backed away from Angelica and then nuzzled Lisa's hand.

"It is not a mystery," said Angelica. "I can tell many things by his body language," she explained. "I could see he missed you by the way he came up next to you when you entered his stall, and by the way he nuzzled you in greeting."

"But what about Jimmy?" asked Lisa. "How did you know Jupiter is afraid of him?"

Instead of answering her, Angelica shut her eyes.

Is she trying to ignore me? thought Lisa, confused. "How did you know about Jimmy?" Lisa repeated her question to Angelica, her voice becoming angry again.

Angelica raised her hand to stop Lisa from speaking and stood for a moment, her eyes still tightly closed. When her amber eyes finally opened, Lisa stepped back. *It's like her eyes are glowing,* she thought. *Like there's a light behind them.*

In one graceful movement, Angelica opened the stall door and grabbed Lisa's hand. Lisa gasped and struggled to pull away, but Angelica's grip, while gentle, was as strong as iron. Before Lisa could object, Angelica had pulled her out of Jupiter's stall and shut his door.

"You must trust me, if only for a moment. Someone is coming," Angelica whispered. "Someone is trying to catch you here."

"Jimmy," said Lisa and stopped struggling. "We've got to hide." Angelica dropped her wrist, and Lisa ran silently toward the large stack of hay bales near the stable door. "I made a hay cave behind here," she explained to Angelica as she squeezed into the narrow crack between the wall and the tall haystack. The stiff hay stalks scratched against her body as she squeezed into the narrow space. Angelica entered the corridor right behind her. The crack widened as they slid along the wall toward the back of the haystack. Lisa had removed some of the hay bales and there was barely enough room for the two of them to stand in the tiny space. Angelica bent her head to stop from hitting the hay that formed the roof of the hay cave.

Lisa sat cross-legged on the loose hay on the floor and leaned back onto a hay bale. "I've been taking the hay from back here to feed the horses," whispered Lisa. "I move the bales at the front of the stack, so I can get the hay out, then I put them back so Jimmy can't tell any are missing."

Suddenly, the stable door crashed open. Angelica spun silently toward the exit as Lisa pulled her legs to her chest and hugged them in a defensive pose. Heavy footfalls sounded to Firefly's stall and then along the line of stalls, stopping for a few seconds in front of each one. At first Lisa couldn't think why Jimmy would stop at each stall, but then it hit her. Jimmy was looking for her.

What if Angelica hadn't heard him in time? she thought as a shiver trickled down her spine. *What if Jimmy called the police and told them I was trespassing? Dad would have been beyond angry with me if the police drove me home. What would he have done to me after they left? But nothing*

21

he could do would be worse than stopping me from taking care of Jupiter. I'm just so glad Angelica showed up tonight of all nights. Maybe she's okay, even though she looks like someone that's escaped from a book of fairy tales.

Lisa drew in a deep breath in relief and lowered her chin to her knees as she exhaled. Then suddenly she sat upright. *What's that?* she wondered. *That smell? Cigarette smoke! Jimmy can't be dumb enough to smoke in a barn full of hay, can he?*

Angelica put her hand on Lisa's shoulder. "Stay here," she whispered. "I am going to see what he is doing."

Lisa watched as Angelica crept closer and closer to the crack between the wall and the haystack. *I can't just sit here,* she thought. Quickly she stood and followed the older girl, trying to move as quietly as Angelica had. It was difficult. The hay seemed to rustle far too loudly with each step. Lisa watched as Angelica reached the end of the narrow tunnel and leaned forward, peering into the main part of the stable. Then she pulled back and turned to Lisa.

"He is beside us, sitting on a bale of hay and leaning on the stack," she whispered so low that Lisa could barely hear her. "And he is smoking a cigarette."

The stupid brat! I know she was here. I heard her talking to that ugly horse of hers. But how did she get out without me seeing her? Not to worry. She's probably just waiting around outside for me to leave, thinking she's got me fooled. She and my uncle are *too* crazy about horses, if you ask me.

I don't see what's so wonderful about the smelly beasts myself. These ones aren't even worth much money. They're just a bunch of pets. The only one that's purebred is that mare—and she's old. I can't wait until I can get rid of them. Should be soon too. If I could just get my hands on that girl, the old man would tell me where it is. I know it.

But I've got to catch her tonight. If I don't, I'm going back to the original plan.

She's as slippery as a shadow too. But she has one weakness: her horse. I know what'll bring her running back in here.

Lisa cringed back against the hay as Jimmy's yell shattered the silence. "Hey little Lisa. Are you listening?" he bellowed. She heard him walk along the line of stalls again. "I know you were here, and I'll bet anything that you can hear me now. I heard you talking to this stupid horse of yours." A whistling noise slashed through the air.

Angelica pulled back into the crevice, her face glowing with anger. "He tried to hit Jupiter!" she breathed.

"What?" said Lisa, a little too loudly.

"Shhhh," whispered Angelica. "He did not hit him. He only tried, but Jupiter is too quick." She turned again to look out into the stable as Jimmy's voice erupted again.

"If you don't come back in here, I'm going to beat your precious black horse," he yelled.

When Lisa heard the loud thump, she started forward, but she couldn't squeeze around Angelica. "Wait," whispered Angelica, but Lisa wasn't listening. She could hear the whistle of the whip slash through the air again, then another thwack as it landed.

"No, he is tricking you. Listen to me!" Angelica's insistent whisper broke through Lisa's anger, and she felt as if a mild electrical current was pushing her backward. "He is hitting a bale of straw with a riding crop," Angelica explained. "He wants to lure you out. He does not know we can see him and is only pretending to beat Jupiter. He wants you to run out to try to save him."

Lisa was so relieved that Jimmy wasn't really beating Jupiter that her knees felt weak. She slumped to the ground as Jimmy continued to whip the bale of hay. She couldn't see him, but she could imagine him with a smile on his face in between the cruel things she could hear him shouting. She hoped he would grow tired of his game soon. Even though she knew he wasn't laying the whip on Jupiter, it still bothered her to hear Jimmy yelling the cruel things he was calling her horse. *Just be patient,* she told herself. *When I don't come, he'll think I was out of hearing range by the time he started.* She plugged her fingers into her ears and tried to concentrate on something else. Anything else.

But at the back of her mind, something nagged at her, though she couldn't think what it was. Jimmy had that effect on her. He made her feel confused and muddle-headed. *Think, think!* she commanded herself. But the only image that came to her mind was Jimmy's narrow face and sly smile, so proud of himself for thinking of luring her back into the stable to save her horse. Enjoying every screamed threat.

Then suddenly, she knew what was bothering her. *How can he be yelling with a cigarette in his mouth?* she wondered. *Can the cigarette be in the hand not holding the whip? Or did he drop it somewhere?*

Lisa stood and touched Angelica on the shoulder, attracting her attention. "The cigarette," she whispered. "What did he do with it?"

Though Angelica's skin was already very fair and they were standing in the shadows, Lisa could still see the older girl's face become even paler. With a shimmer of golden hair, Angelica looked around the edge of the haystack. In a moment, she pulled back and turned to Lisa. "He no longer has it," she whispered.

"We've got to find it," insisted Lisa. "What if it's laying in a bit of straw somewhere? Or even worse, has landed on the haystack? Or maybe it's in one of the stalls? The entire stable could be burned to the ground."

Angelica just nodded as she turned again to peer out the crack. Lisa waited behind her as she searched the stable. Jimmy was growing tired of pretending to beat Jupiter and his obscenities were fading away. Lisa noticed Angelica flinch as her eyes roamed the stable floor.

"Did you find it?" whispered Lisa. At first Angelica didn't seem to hear her. Then she pulled back into the crevice with a slight intake of breath.

"Yes," she whispered. "It is in front of Firefly's stall and is smoking still. We are going to have to put it out somehow and as soon as we can. It is much too close to the haystack. If it ever ignited the hay…." The end of Angelica's sentence faded away into nothing, suggesting something too horrible to say and to hear. But Lisa knew how devastating the results could be. All the horses could be killed. Burned alive. She and Angelica were close to the door and could easily escape, but the horses would be trapped.

"How are we going to put it out when we have to hide in here," asked Lisa, her whispered words hinged on the edge of panic. *If the haystack starts on fire, we should try to get Firefly first,* she thought, already planning ahead. *She's the closest to the haystack. Maybe Angelica could get Firefly, and I could open the other horse's stalls and get Jupiter. But what about Jimmy? Is he so angry he would even stop us from saving the horses? Even he couldn't be that awful, could he?*

"Just one minute," whispered Angelica, interrupting Lisa's thoughts. "I have an idea, but you have to turn around. I do not want you to see what I am going to do."

27

"Whaa…" Lisa started to say, but then she realized there was no time. She would have to trust Angelica. She turned and faced the little hay cave. With the stable wall on one side and the hay wall close to her other side, Lisa couldn't see anything behind her, even out of the corner of her eye. Though she couldn't see Angelica at all, Lisa could still hear and strained her ears for sounds of Angelica's movements.

At first there was nothing. Then a noise grew out of the silence so gradually it was as if the sound had always been there, just waiting to rise into the normal level of hearing. It was like singing and like the wind and like the water rushing along a rocky streambed all braided into one noise, but so hushed and so soft that Lisa felt a wave of peace flow over her. Somewhere in the back of her mind, she noticed that Jimmy seemed to become louder and angrier.

A loud bang struck through the peaceful noise, and Lisa started. As she spun around, another loud crack filled the air, and then Lisa heard Jimmy muttering as he moved toward Firefly's stall.

"What did you do?" whispered Lisa.

"Nothing," Angelica whispered back. "I did not have time."

"Then what was that noise," asked Lisa.

"Firefly kicked the door of her stall," explained Angelica. "And now Jimmy is walking toward her. Maybe he will notice the cigarette."

Lisa flinched as the sound of Jimmy's whip whistled through the air. His loud voice screamed at the mare and Firefly's hooves echoed on the hard floor as she spun away, trying to avoid being struck.

"Stupid horses," muttered Jimmy. Then Lisa heard his footsteps come toward them. Angelica pulled back as he came to within three feet of their hiding place. Lisa shut her eyes. Then she heard the door slam shut.

Angelica turned toward her. "Stay here," she whispered. "He may not go far and only one of us should risk being caught." She slipped from the narrow corridor and ran toward the smoking cigarette. Within seconds it was out, crushed underfoot, and ground to powder. Then Angelica slipped to the stable door without uttering a sound. She turned out the light before opening it just a crack and looking into the night. "Stay here," she whispered to Lisa, then opened the door a little wider and slipped through, pulling the door closed behind her. Lisa waited as the longest minute of her life slowly ticked past. She hardly noticed she was holding her breath until the door opened and Angelica slipped back into the stable.

"He has gone back inside the house," Angelica said aloud to Lisa as she locked the stable door behind her and switched on the light. "We are safe for now."

Lisa stepped out from the narrow corridor and hurried to Firefly's stall. "Are you okay, girl?" she asked. "Did he hurt you?" Firefly approached Lisa and buried her nose in Lisa's hands. "You're okay," Lisa murmured. "I was so worried about all of you." She walked down the line of stalls checking each horse in turn. Finally, she stopped at Jupiter's stall. Jupiter nuzzled her as she stroked his neck.

"Why does he feel so much hatred for you?" Angelica asked Lisa. She had stopped at Topper's stall and was trying to comfort the grey gelding as he paced back and forth.

"I don't know. He doesn't want me on the property at all, and I don't understand why," said Lisa. She kicked her foot lightly against the stall door. "I mean, I help with the horses and feed and water them and clean their stalls, all for free," she continued. "And I turn them out and bring them in again after they've had a run. He doesn't want me to do it, but then he doesn't do it himself. Look at Jupiter's trough. He didn't even feed him tonight, even though he fed Firefly. I didn't check the others, but I'm guessing he fed them too, but not Jupiter. It's just not fair."

Now that she had started, Lisa had a hard time stopping. There had been no one to tell her worries to except the horses and it felt so nice to have someone to confide in. "The horses haven't been turned out to run for days, and they're going crazy. He never cleans their stalls and I'm never sure how much to clean. I mean, I don't want him to know how much I come over or when, so I always have to leave the stalls a little bit dirty. And Mr. Pickering has been sick. I haven't been able to talk to him for ages. I know he liked me to help before Jimmy came, and he's a great old guy. He wouldn't like the way Jimmy is taking care of the horses if he knew."

"And Jimmy is so scary," Lisa continued as Angelica put her arm around her and led her toward the bale of straw that Jimmy had beaten. Angelica sat down and Lisa sat beside her. "He drinks a lot and I think he's been hitting the horses, not just pretending like he did tonight. I know Jupiter is scared of him. But I can't phone the police because I'm not supposed to be here."

"And your mother and father?" asked Angelica. "Why do you not tell them what is happening?"

"That's part of the problem. My dad said I wasn't allowed to come here ever again. He would be so mad if he knew I had been sneaking over. He hates Mr. Pickering just because he bought our house. He told me I had to forget about Jupiter, but how can I do that when he needs me? Jupie won't eat unless I feed him. He was getting better and beginning to trust Mr. Pickering and everything seemed to be okay. Not great but okay. And then Jimmy came and everything got a lot worse." She paused for a moment and tore at

30

the bale of straw with her fingers. Angelica was quiet, waiting for her to continue.

"You see, Jupiter was orphaned as a foal," explained Lisa. "I saved his life when he was a baby, and he's still dependent on me even now that he's big. On days like today, it's really hard when I can't come until everyone is in bed and Jupiter has to wait for me to feed him. He's lost a lot of weight since Jimmy got here." She looked up at Angelica. "You won't tell anyone what I've said, will you?" she asked, suddenly nervous. "If my dad found out, I would never be able to come back again."

"I will not tell," Angelica reassured her. "And maybe I can even help you."

"What do you mean?" asked Lisa hopefully.

"I could take care of the horses in the mornings," offered Angelica. "Then they will have food and water all day, and you do not have to worry about them until nightfall. And if you cannot come at night, I can come then too. I am near the stables."

"Near the stables?" repeated Lisa.

"I am staying nearby," answered Angelica. "I can be at the stable in a few minutes from my place, and I would love to help you take care of the horses. I do not go to school so it will be easier for me."

"That would be wonderful," said Lisa and smiled at Angelica. "I saw that Jupiter likes you, so he might even eat the food you give him. It helps so much to know someone will help me take care of them and that someone else cares about them. Watch out for Jimmy though. He's really scary. He's a bad person. I can just tell. I don't know how else to say it, but he really gives me the creeps."

"I will be careful," promised Angelica. "Do not worry. I can be pretty sneaky too."

31

Lisa smiled. It felt so good to have someone share the responsibility of the horses' well being, someone who obviously cared for them and understood them. "Come on, I'll introduce you to everyone and show you what we need to do. My name is Lisa, by the way. You probably know all the horse's names by the nameplates on their stalls, but this is Firefly. That's Topper. Here is Dakota. And you've already met Jupiter."

Lisa showed Angelica where the grain was kept and where the fork and wheelbarrow were kept for cleaning the stalls. As Jupiter happily munched his grain, she showed Angelica how she cleaned the stall. First she removed all the dirty bedding and replaced it with clean straw. They had to take a bale from the back of the pile, so Jimmy wouldn't notice any of the straw bales were missing. Then she spread the fresh bedding on the stall floor.

"Then usually I take a tiny bit of the dirty straw and sprinkle it on top, just enough to make the bedding look used. I know it doesn't make much sense to throw dirty straw back down, but I don't know how else to make the bedding look like it hasn't been changed. I don't think we need to do it tonight though. Obviously Jimmy already knows I was here."

"I would like to see his face when he sees the clean stalls tomorrow morning," said Angelica. "Then he will know you were not frightened of him. He will know you came back."

"If he even comes into the stable in the morning," said Lisa. "Sometimes he doesn't take care of the horses for a whole day at a time. They get so hungry and thirsty. And the strange thing is, he doesn't turn them out even though it would be a lot less work for him. It's almost like he forgets they exist."

When they were finished with Jupiter's stall, Angelica

moved on to Topper's stall and Lisa started working in Dakota's. The black and gray-spotted Appaloosa pony nosed Lisa as she worked. "I know you want to get out, boy," she said. "Maybe tomorrow you'll have a chance."

Angelica moved on to Firefly's stall as soon as Topper's straw was spotless, and Lisa began to brush the horses and pick their hooves. As soon as Angelica was done she began to help with the grooming. Soon all four horses were clean and content. Jupiter was finishing the last of his hay. When Lisa went to his stall door, he sighed contentedly. Angelica came up beside her. "He loves you so much," she said to Lisa. "I can see it in his eyes."

"He likes you too," said Lisa. "I'm amazed at how relaxed he is with you in the stable. He took weeks to get used to Mr. Pickering, and he's already more relaxed around you after just one night. It's amazing."

Angelica smiled and stroked Jupiter's face. "Some have said I have a way with horses."

"You do," replied Lisa. "And to me, that's the biggest compliment a person can give."

"Thanks," said Angelica.

"See you tomorrow, Jupie," Lisa whispered and kissed the black gelding on the nose. "You sleep well tonight, and I should be able to come visit sometime tomorrow."

"I will be here early, so do not worry if you cannot come until later," said Angelica.

"Thanks."

Lisa led Angelica back the way she had come. The entire house was dark now. The lights had been turned off in the library as well, but Lisa could still see dark heaps on the floor in the glow of the almost full moon. She knew they must be the books Jimmy had been throwing down.

I thought Mr. Pickering stopped him from trashing the li-

brary, thought Lisa when she noticed there were a lot more books scattered on the floor than when she went by the library earlier. She frowned. *Why didn't Mr. Pickering stop him?* wondered Lisa. *Did he want Jimmy to look through all the books? I'm going to talk to Mr. Pickering tomorrow even if I have to go up to the front door and risk Jimmy answering the doorbell. I have to find out what's going on.*

Suddenly Lisa's thoughts were pulled away from the mess in the library. "Did you hear that?" she whispered to Angelica. She could hear the strange humming noise again. Lisa closed her eyes and tried to concentrate, but she still couldn't define what the sound was or even which direction it was coming from. It was there for only a few seconds and then slowly, slowly, it disappeared into the stillness of the night. She heard a thump come from the stable and looked back into the darkness.

"Do not worry," whispered Angelica in a soft voice. "One of the horses kicked at their stall once more."

"They're getting so tired of being inside," Lisa whispered back just as quietly. "Maybe tomorrow, after I talk to Mr. Pickering, we can let them out in the pasture to run for a while."

In a few minutes, they reached Lisa's house and crept into the back yard. A dog barked twice and Lisa jumped. "Neptune. Be quiet," she commanded the German Shepherd. Neptune whined apologetically when he realized who it was and came forward to greet them, his tail wagging back and forth. Before Lisa climbed into her bedroom window, she turned back to Angelica.

"Thanks again," she whispered. "I'm so glad the horses have both of us now."

"Me too. I will see you tomorrow," whispered Angelica in reply.

34

"Hey, where is your house?" asked Lisa. "You said before that you lived nearby."

"Do not worry," said Angelica. "I do not have far to walk." Then she stepped back into the night.

"Remember to be careful of Jimmy tomorrow," said Lisa as she turned back toward her window. When there was no reply, she looked behind her. Her eyes searched the darkness for Angelica, but all she could see was the dog's black form against the lawn.

"Neptune?" she whispered. The dog's paws whispered against the grass as he walked toward her. His soft panting seemed loud in the stillness. But she hadn't heard Angelica walk away or seen her retreat across the lawn into the darkness. She was just gone.

That was a close call. I do not think Lisa realized Jimmy was so near, waiting for us in the shadows. He knew we were there somewhere and was searching for us. I am glad Lisa knows to be nervous of him. Jimmy not only does not care when he hurts others, but even worse, he enjoys their pain. He is a dangerous man who has let evil overcome him.

Thankfully Jupiter saved us tonight by kicking the door of his stall and distracting Jimmy. I hope Jimmy is not too hard on him. I hope he thinks it was Firefly. He seems to value her above the others. His attempt to strike her earlier was only half-hearted.

Tomorrow I will find out more. I must discover Jimmy's plan before it is too late.

"Jupie!" The word burst from Lisa's lips as she woke with a start. She had been dreaming that Jupiter was calling her. Neighing to her to come to him. *No,* she thought. *Not neighing. He was screaming.*

She sat up in bed, breathing heavily, then slowly reached up and covered her face with her hands. *It was just a dream,* she reminded herself. She couldn't remember what she had seen in her dream, but the sound of Jupiter's screams seemed glued to the inside of her brain. And there had been another voice too. Her dad's deep rumble telling her she would never see Jupiter again. That he was gone forever. Lisa raised her head. "It was just a stupid dream," she said aloud.

She stood and walked to the window. It was early morning and the sunlight across the back lawn was weak and rose-colored. Neptune was lying outside his doghouse staring into the sunrise, an absent look in his eyes. Behind her, the house was still. No one was awake yet. Lisa smiled. *I don't have to rush off to see the horses this morning,* she remembered with pleasure. *Angelica is taking care of them for me.* With a yawn, she walked back to her bed and climbed under the covers, pushed the nightmare firmly out of her mind, and shut her eyes.

It was late morning when she awoke the second time. Lisa stretched. She felt much more rested and relaxed. Her eyes opened, and she stared at the bright carpet for a few seconds, then shut them again. *Just a few more minutes,* she thought. *I'll lay here for just a few more minutes.*

Slowly, the noises of the house crept into her room. Cartoons were playing on the TV in the living room. She heard Molly run past her room and then her sister's bedroom door slam shut. The loud bang made her think of Firefly kicking the wall of her stall. Then Molly opened and shut the door again. Her footsteps softly thudded past Lisa's room as she ran toward the living room. Lisa breathed deeply and stretched again. *It's time to get up anyway,* she thought. *But it's been a wonderful morning. This is the first time I've slept in for weeks.*

Lisa's eyes opened again and she stared at the ceiling as her thoughts continued. *I wonder why I haven't seen Angelica around the neighborhood. I know I would have remembered her if I saw her before. There's something about her that's different, very different. She's so...strange! And it's more than the fact she's the most beautiful person I've seen in my whole life. I should ask her where she comes from. Or even more important, find out how she understands horses. I'd love to talk to Jupiter like she does.*

"Lisa?" a tiny voice came from the other side of her bedroom door. Lisa turned over and pulled the covers over her head, hoping Molly would think she was asleep and not come in. To her dismay, she heard the door open. *I need to get a lock on my door,* she thought in frustration.

"Lisa?" said Molly again, this time a little louder. Lisa held still and breathed deeply, trying to sound like she was asleep.

"Lisa, it's time to get up," her mom said from the doorway.

Lisa finally turned over. Molly was standing at the bed with a hopeful expression on her face. "I'm up, Mom," Lisa said and grimaced at her little sister. Molly looked down at the floor and immediately Lisa felt bad. *She's just lonely,* she realized. *She wants to spend time with me. Everything that's been happening in the family has been hard on her too.* "Hey Molly," Lisa said in a lighter voice as she pushed herself into a sitting position. "What's up?"

Molly looked at her shyly. "Can we go for a walk?" she asked.

"But I just woke up," Lisa protested.

"That sounds like a wonderful idea, Molly," said their mom. "I'm sure Lisa would love to go for a walk with you."

"Yeah, I'd love to," said Lisa trying to sound cheerful, though she knew she'd rather do almost anything else. "Just let me get dressed first. You go get your shoes on and wait for me by the door." She flopped back in bed and listened as Molly's feet thudded along the floor as she ran toward the front door. With a groan, Lisa threw the covers back and got out of bed.

"Your dad just left," said Lisa's mom. "He decided to leave a bit earlier than he had planned."

"That's too bad," answered Lisa, trying to keep the relief out of her voice.

Lisa was ready to go in a couple of minutes. She met Molly at the door and began to help her on with her windbreaker. Her 4-year-old sister pushed her away.

"I'm big now, Lisa," she said. "I do it myself." She pushed her short arms into the jacket and then tried to zip it up. Lisa had to help her fit the bottom of the zipper together, then Molly pulled the zipper upward along its track. "Let's go to the pond, Lisa," she said. "I want to see the frogs."

"No, we can't go to the pond," Lisa said in an impatient voice. "I've told you a thousand times, the pond belongs to Mr. Pickering now, not to us. We can climb the hill instead.

That way you can see the pond down below. That's the closest we can get."

"But I want to play in the pond," whined Molly. "And I want to see D'kota."

Lisa looked up, silently imploring her mother to help her. "Lisa's right," said their mom to Molly. "Maybe you can go to the pond on another day."

"Then we can climb the big hill?" asked Molly.

"Sure," said Lisa holding out her hand. "We can take Neptune with us. You can even hold his leash if you want." As she followed her little sister outside, Lisa grabbed Neptune's leash from beside the door.

Within a few minutes they were at the base of the hill. Lisa helped Molly through the fence and together they climbed along the gently sloping trail that switch backed to the top. The hill was part of the land belonging to their neighbors, a young couple doing their best to make a go of sheep farming. As long as Lisa kept Neptune on his leash, they didn't mind that Lisa and Molly went onto their land. Lisa loved the view from the top of the hill. Her neighbor's sheep looked so peaceful grazing in their green pastures. They always made her feel calmer, even on her most stressed days.

On the other side of the hilltop, the view stretched over Evergreen Manor and its surrounding paddocks. Lisa could have spent hours staring over the green pastures and the big white house if she had the time. Except for being with horses, climbing the hill on a sunny day was her favorite thing to do. She would look over the land that had been her home, then read a few passages from whichever book she had decided to bring with her that day. When she looked back at the scene stretched before her, it's beauty startled her: the velvet pastures, the horses grazing when Mr. Pickering had them turned out, the house glowing in the sunlight, the trees swaying in the breeze. Every time it was as if she was seeing it for the first time. Now and then she even smelled the perfume from the rose garden behind the house. It was as if the wind was involved in a plot with Mr. Pickering to always make her feel wanted at her former home.

Right from the beginning, Mr. Pickering had made her feel welcome. The first day he moved in, Lisa gathered her courage and rang his doorbell. When Mr. Pickering came to the door, he seemed happy to meet her. After she explained that she needed to help Jupiter learn to trust him, he asked her if she would help him take care of all the horses. Because of his arthritis, he explained, he couldn't ride and he asked Lisa if she would be interested in riding the horses, one each day. Lisa had been overjoyed. For a few golden weeks during the summer, she spent every spare minute at Mr. Pickering's house.

She and Mr. Pickering became fast friends. He had had an interesting life, full of adventure and travel. He told her of the places he had been and the people and horses he had met. He recommended books for her to read and every time Lisa finished one, the two of them would discuss the author's words in detail. At first Lisa wondered if it was right for her to enjoy his company so much, but then she decided he was like a grandpa or a favorite uncle.

But when her dad found out about her friendship with the old man, the idyllic summer days became a thing of the past. Then Jimmy had showed up at Mr. Pickering's door, and right after that Mr. Pickering became ill. Everything changed immediately. Lisa wasn't welcome at Evergreen Manor anymore. The horses were rarely turned into the pastures and were forced to stand in dirty stalls, day after day, sometimes without food or water. *He makes me so mad,* thought Lisa as she followed Molly up the hill, allowing her to travel at her own speed. *I wish he would just go away, back to the city or wherever he came from. I wish he would just disappear!*

"Look!" said Molly's excited voice as she reached the top of the hill. She pointed toward Evergreen Manor. "D'kota! And Juter and Firefie and Topper."

Lisa turned toward the Manor. Molly was right. The four horses were grazing peacefully in the paddock in front of the house. As they watched, Jupiter raised his head and whinnied. He galloped toward the fence where a lone figure stood. Even from a distance, Lisa could see Angelica's golden hair flashing in the sunlight. Jupiter slowed to a trot as he came close to the fence, then spun away. Molly giggled beside Lisa and reached out to hug Neptune. Firefly was the next to approach and then ran away. When Dakota trotted to Angelica, he pushed his muzzle into her hands and then backed away bobbing his head.

Molly laughed as she watched the horses' antics. "They want the angel to come play with them," she said, giggling.

"What do you mean Molly?" asked Lisa in a startled voice. "She's not an angel."

"Yes she is!" insisted Molly. "I know she is. She's an angel for horses."

"She's not an angel, Molly," said Lisa, impatiently. "Don't be silly! She's a girl like you and me." She watched Angelica slip through the boards of the fence and begin to play with the horses. First she ran toward Jupiter and, when he wheeled away, she spun around and raced in the opposite direction as quick as a deer. Jupiter was puzzled and turned to follow her. When Angelica stopped with her back to him, he quietly walked up behind her. He touched her shoulder with his muzzle and she turned toward him, laughing. The sound of her laughter was like tiny silver bells tinkling in the distance.

Lisa drew in her breath when Angelica leaped onto the black gelding's back and they began to race around the paddock. The other horses—red chestnut, iron gray and leopard Appaloosa—leaped and jumped behind them, joyfully stretching their legs and tossing their heads. Lisa couldn't take her eyes off Jupiter as his legs skimmed over the ground. He was so beautiful! So glorious!

"Her hair is funny," said Molly and pulled Neptune even closer to her.

Lisa hadn't looked closely at Angelica; her eyes had been so full of the beautiful horse that had once been hers. She focused on the girl clinging to his back and then blinked her eyes. "It must be an optical illusion," she murmured, more to herself than to her little sister. Angelica's hair still shimmered in the sunlight, but it shimmered black, not gold. It was so long that the ends of it trailed over Jupiter's back, blending in perfectly with his broad, black back.

"What's optal lusions?" asked Molly.

"Not optal lusions, Molly," said Lisa, looking down at her little sister. "Optical illusion. Optical means what you can see with your eyes, and illusion means something that looks like something else. So an optical illusion is when you see something that looks different from what it really is. You know, like a mirage in the desert," she explained.

"What's mirror adje?" asked Molly.

"Never mind," said Lisa and looked back at the horses. They had stopped running and Angelica was back on the ground, her hair looking as golden as ever.

"No, Lisa, tell me. What's a mirror adje?" insisted Molly.

"I'll tell you what a mirage is as we walk down the hill," said Lisa. "I have lots of things to do today besides take you and Neptune for walks." *And I can hardly wait to see Jupiter,* she thought. *He looked so wonderful running around! And Jimmy must be gone if Angelica is standing in the open like that. Hopefully Mr. Pickering is home so I can finally talk to him.*

Lisa tried to hurry Molly along, but it seemed to take forever to climb down the hill. Once they reached the bottom, Molly dawdled along, pulling seeds off the tall grass stalks and throwing them into the air. "I'm a farmer," she kept saying. "I'm planting corn! Neptune is my cow!" By the time they reached the house, Lisa felt like she was going to burst, either from frustration at Molly's slowness or from holding back her laughter at her little sister's game.

"Why don't you go get your paints and paint a picture of Dakota running around the pasture," suggested Lisa to her little sister, when they walked into the kitchen.

"Will you paint with me, Lisa?" said Molly. "You can paint Juter and the angel."

"I told you Molly, she's not an angel and, no, I can't paint

45

now. I have to go out for a while," Lisa said as she grabbed some paper and a pen from the junk drawer. She began to write a note for her mom saying she was going to visit a friend.

It's not really a lie, she reasoned as she penned the words. *Jupiter is my friend and so is Mr. Pickering.* She could hear her mom moving around in the laundry room and hurried to finish the note. She felt bad sneaking out before her mom came into the kitchen, but she knew if she asked her if she could go, her mom would probably have some more chores for her to do. *And I've got to get over there while the horses are still outside,* reasoned Lisa. *I haven't ridden Jupiter for ages. I can always help Mom this afternoon. I won't even wait for her to ask me.*

After a hurried good-bye to Molly, Lisa rushed out the front door and began to run down the driveway. At the road, she turned toward Evergreen Manor and within a couple of minutes, reached the large front gate. She peeked through the gate but couldn't tell if Jimmy was there or not. His car wasn't in front of the Manor, but she knew it could be in the garage or around the back of the house as well.

Angelica and the horses were in plain sight. Angelica stood with her back to the Manor, leaning on the fence and watching the horses. They were grazing peacefully again, switching their tails at the occasional fly and enjoying the autumn grass.

Angelica and Jupiter saw Lisa at the same time. Angelica waved to her to come over and Jupiter began to trot toward her, his head and tail high in the air. Lisa slipped through the fence bordering the driveway and ran toward him.

"Jupie," she whispered in his ear when he shoved his coal black head down so she could pet him. "You are so beautiful and I am so glad you live right next door, if you can't be my

46

own." The black gelding nickered to her and Lisa hugged him around the neck. "We're so lucky it was Mr. Pickering that bought our house and not someone like Jimmy." She twisted her fingers in his long silky mane and the two of them walked together toward Angelica.

"Good morning," she said shyly to the older girl.

"It is a wonderful morning," agreed Angelica and smiled. She was even more beautiful in the daylight and Lisa wondered again why she hadn't seen Angelica in the neighborhood before. *She must have just moved here because otherwise I would have noticed her,* she thought. *She's like a movie star or something. Only prettier. No wonder Molly thinks she's an angel.*

"Where's Jimmy?" asked Lisa, dropping her eyes.

"He left early this morning. Alone. I do not know where Mr. Pickering is," replied Angelica. "There has been no sign of movement from inside the house, and no one came out to take care of the horses."

"He probably knew that I'd take care of them, so he didn't bother," said Lisa and turned toward Jupiter to pet him. "I'm going to try to talk to Mr. Pickering today though, if he's not too sick to come to the door. I wanted to ask him about Jimmy, and it's the perfect opportunity now that Jimmy's gone. He'll like to see the horses too. They looked so beautiful running this morning that I'm sure they'll make him feel better."

"You saw them running?" asked Angelica, looking at her with tawny eyes.

Lisa nodded. "I took my little sister for a walk to the top of that hill," she said pointing. "Molly thinks you're an angel," she added and laughed, but even to her own ears, the laugh sounded forced.

Angelica noticed the strain in Lisa's voice. "What is wrong?" she asked, her face serious.

47

At first Lisa didn't know what to say. *How can I tell her that she makes me nervous?* she wondered. *There is so much energy around her, it's almost as if she glows sometimes. And how can I say that she's so beautiful she actually looks like she could be an angel if she had wings. The only thing that doesn't scare me very much is that she can talk to horses. I've heard of horse whisperers before.*

"You do not need to feel uncomfortable around me, Lisa," Angelica quietly continued. "I am here to help you. I know I may not seem like a normal person but ..."

"You're so pretty," interrupted Lisa. It seemed the safest of the strange things to mention to Angelica.

"Do not remind me. It is not that great being pretty. Believe me," said Angelica as she raised an eyebrow. When Lisa looked at her with a doubtful face, Angelica laughed. "I am serious," she said. "Just imagine what it is like to have everyone look at you no matter where you are or who you are with. I cannot go anywhere or do anything without everyone noticing me. Some people like me too much and other people act like they hate me, all because of the way I look. And neither are that interested in getting to know me. You know, the *real* person that I am. That is why I like horses so much. They do not care what I look like."

Lisa looked at the ground as she thought about what Angelica had said. *She's right,* Lisa finally decided. *Even I was suspicious of her because of the way she looks. But not anymore.* She looked up. "Sorry."

"Hey, I am glad you are honest with me," said Angelica. "Most people do not think to ask how I feel about the way I look. They do not realize how difficult it is!"

Lisa laughed. She liked Angelica's sense of humor too.

"Did you see me ride Jupiter?" asked Angelica, reaching out to stroke the black neck.

"Yeah, and without a saddle or a bridle," said Lisa. "How did you do that?"

"It is easy," answered Angelica. "I can tell you how. Do you want to try?"

Lisa swallowed. She trusted Jupiter more than any horse in the world but she had never ridden without a saddle or bridle before. What if she fell off?

"He will be careful," said Angelica. When Jupiter snorted, she leaned over and kissed him on the face. "He promises," she added to Lisa.

"Okay," said Lisa and waited for Angelica to climb through the fence and give her a boost onto Jupiter's broad back. Once aboard, Lisa grabbed at his mane.

"He is easy to free-ride," said Angelica, patting Jupiter on the shoulder. "He reacts to all of the leg aids to turn or go faster and you can use "whoa" to ask him to stop."

Lisa signalled to Jupiter to turn to the left. Smoothly he walked into the pasture. Firefly, Topper and Dakota began to file along behind him as Angelica climbed back through the fence. She leaned on the top rail and watched them walk into the center of the field, then called to Lisa. "Hey Lisa, I am going to go ring the doorbell for Mr. Pickering. I am sure he would like to watch you free-ride Jupiter."

Lisa turned and looked back. "He would love see them all. Maybe I'll even get Jupie to trot," she yelled and then straightened on the black gelding's back. She asked Jupiter to turn to the left again and the other horses followed him in a large arc. By the time they were walking toward the house again, Angelica was almost at the front door. Lisa watched her climb the few steps onto the small porch and ring the doorbell.

"Whoa," Lisa said to Jupiter when they were back where they had started. She watched Angelica standing at the door for a minute, but the door didn't open. *Would Mr. Pickering*

be sleeping this late? she wondered. *Or is he just too sick today? No, he must be asleep. Jimmy wouldn't have left if Mr. Pickering was very sick. Jimmy may be a jerk but even he's not that clueless.*

Lisa turned Jupiter into the pasture again. She let him walk along the fence line for a few steps then urged him into a trot. Jupiter sprang forward, and Lisa grabbed onto his mane. Then she asked him to canter. The bouncing trot ended abruptly as Jupiter flowed into a slow, steady canter. He tucked his head in as if he was wearing a bridle and was collected, even without Lisa having reins to use.

"You are such a good horse, Jupie," said Lisa leaning forward. Suddenly Firefly raced up on Jupiter's left and passed them. Immediately Jupiter broke into a gallop. Lisa felt her heart begin to pound faster, matching Jupiter's racing hoofbeats. She clung low over his neck, her white knuckles gripping his mane. His black hair whipped into her face making her eyes sting. Now Topper was alongside them too, slowly surging ahead as they turned the corner and continued to gallop along the fence. Jupiter was having none of that. His body stretched low to the ground as he moved from a gallop into a full run.

For a moment, Lisa was terrified but then she began to feel Jupiter's excitement. He was giving her the ride of her life. She clung to his back like a burr and urged him on. Slowly, they began to gain on Topper. By the time they reached the turn in the fence, they were ahead of him. Firefly's red hindquarters were in front of them, her tail streaming out in the wind.

"Go Jupie," yelled Lisa. It was all the encouragement he needed. With a last burst of speed, he drew alongside the chestnut mare. For a moment they were running neck and neck, black and red, then the black pulled ahead.

51

"Whoa, Jupie," said Lisa calmly. "Whoa now. We've won. Whoa." The black gelding began to slow and soon he was cantering, then trotting, and finally walking. Lisa turned him back toward the gate and all the horses turned with her. Sweat beaded their shoulders and they were all breathing heavily. Angelica was back at the gate and stood watching them approach.

"That was amazing!" said Lisa when they reached Angelica. She laughed out loud as she slid from Jupiter's back. "I can't believe how fantastic it was! I've got to do that more often!"

Lisa stopped talking when she noticed the serious look on Angelica's face. "What's wrong?" she asked.

"Mr. Pickering did not come to the door," said Angelica.

"Couldn't that mean he's just sleeping?" asked Lisa.

Angelica's face relaxed slightly. "Maybe I worry too much," she replied, but Lisa noticed that her eyes were still concerned.

"Maybe we could try again in a little while," suggested Lisa. "Jimmy wouldn't have left him here if there was anything wrong."

Angelica looked at Lisa for a moment as if trying to decide what to do. Finally she nodded her head. "We could clean the stable while we wait. It's a good time since the horses are outside."

Lisa agreed. "Let's do a really good job again too. It'll be nice to see the horses in clean stalls for two days in a row."

"I agree," said Angelica with a smile.

It took almost two hours to thoroughly clean the stable. After Lisa finished sweeping the aisle in front of the stalls, she looked around with pride. The stalls had been cleaned and filled with sweet smelling bedding, the troughs filled with a light lunch for the horses, the floor of the stable swept clean of any stray hay wisps, and the tack had been cleaned and neatly organized in the tack room. Lisa sighed contently. It was nice to see the stable look and smell the way it should.

Angelica emerged from the tack room with a grooming

kit in her hand. "I am going to start brushing the horses," she said as she moved toward the stable door.

"Good idea," said Lisa. "I'll be out in a minute to help." She hung the broom in the tack room, then moved to each stall and opened the doors in preparation for bringing the horses in from the pasture. Finally, she grabbed a horse blanket from the tack room and carried it into their little cave in the haystack. She pushed back the loose hay on the floor of their hay cave with her foot, leaving the center of their hideout clean and bare, and then arranged the horse blanket over one of the bales of hay.

Just as she was about to leave the stable, Lisa paused and looked back. The stable was so peaceful and fresh and pretty. *I wish I had appreciated this place when I lived here,* she thought. *I didn't realize how lucky I was then.* With a sad shake of her head, she walked outside, pulling the door shut behind her.

Angelica was busy brushing Dakota. The little Appaloosa pony was enjoying being pampered. He stretched out his neck and closed his eyes as Angelica used the body brush to loosen the dirt and dust from his coat. Lisa grabbed another body brush and began to groom Jupiter. Soon his coat was glistening, and his mane and tail were tangle-free and smooth. The silky hair fluttered in the slight breeze. Angelica finished with Dakota and moved on to Topper, leaving Firefly for Lisa to groom. Quietly they worked side by side, both comfortable in their silence, while the horses dozed.

When they were finally finished, Lisa glanced at her watch. "I can't believe it's so late," she said in surprise. "It's almost 2 p.m. Today has just been so much fun that time has disappeared."

"I know," agreed Angelica. "I enjoyed it too." She untied both Dakota and Topper and led them toward the stable.

"Do you have to go home soon?" she asked over her shoulder.

"Yeah," replied Lisa. "I have to help my mom with some chores around the house this afternoon, but I hope I can come back tonight after I finish my homework." She untied Firefly and Jupiter and led them behind the other two horses.

The horses were glad to see their lunch waiting for them in the clean stalls. When Lisa led Jupiter into his stall he buried his nose in his oats with vigor. "It's so nice to see him eating well again," said Lisa. "I was starting to get worried about him."

Angelica laughed. "Well he is certainly trying to catch up on the food he has missed," she said. "He is acting as if he has not eaten for a week."

When Angelica and Lisa moved to leave, there were no whinnies of farewell. The horses' mouths were too full, and they were concentrating on their oats.

After another unsuccessful attempt to wake Mr. Pickering, Lisa and Angelica walked up the driveway. "What time are you coming back tonight?" asked Angelica, finally breaking the silence when they reached the road.

"I can probably come around 11 p.m. Dad's gone and Mom will be in bed by then for sure," said Lisa. "It'll be an easy night to get out."

"Lisa, if we cannot speak to Mr. Pickering soon, we will have to tell someone about him being sick and alone. Something may have happened to him," said Angelica. When Lisa nodded in agreement, Angelica continued. "And they will probably tell your mother and father."

Lisa looked down at the ground. "My dad will be so mad with me," she said in a quiet voice. "They would both start watching me all the time and I wouldn't be able to get out to see Jupiter anymore. Who would take care of him then?"

"If Mr. Pickering is hurt, we need to get help for him," said Angelica. "What if he has fallen? What if he needs medicine?"

Lisa's face grew a little paler and she was silent for a moment. "Couldn't we sneak into the house and see for ourselves?" she finally asked, her voice strained. "Since Jimmy's gone it would be easy to do. Even if they tried to lock all the windows and doors, I'm sure I could find a way inside. Then we could check on Mr. Pickering ourselves."

"If he is resting and finds us in his house, would he not be angry?" asked Angelica. "Would he not telephone your mother and father anyway?"

"Hey, that's it. I could try to phone him," suggested Lisa. "He probably has a phone by his bed."

"Okay," agreed Angelica. "Tell me tonight what you find out and, if you cannot talk to him, we will make a new plan. Do you want me to meet you outside your house?"

"Sure, I'll see you at 11 p.m.," replied Lisa as she turned away. But she didn't step forward. When she didn't hear Angelica walk away from her, she turned back. "Do you really think something may have happened to him?" she asked, her voice barely above a whisper and her eyes grave.

Angelica looked sad. "I do not know," she said softly. "But there is something wrong. What it is I cannot tell yet." She paused and looked deep into Lisa's eyes. "Is there something you want to tell me?"

Lisa tried to turn away from the golden eyes but she couldn't. She felt mesmerized, entranced, as if Angelica was pulling the truth from her. "It's nothing," she finally stammered. "I'm sure it's nothing."

"What is this nothing?" asked Angelica.

"I'll tell you tonight," said Lisa. "Maybe. I can't tell you now. I need to think first. I need to think if it's even that important."

Angelica looked at her for a long moment, then finally nodded. Lisa forced herself to turn toward home. She kicked the ground as she hurried away, rolling tiny rocks in front of her. Once she almost turned back to call Angelica to wait. To tell her she wanted to talk about it right then. *But no!* she commanded herself at the last instant. *Dad couldn't have done anything to Mr. Pickering.* From the back of her mind, the idea rose, an unwelcome thought. *But Dad left earlier than usual this morning. Could it be because he knew Jimmy was going to be gone? Did my dad really mean what he said on the patio? And even if he did mean it, he wouldn't really hurt Mr. Pickering, would he?*

Lisa's thoughts turned back two nights to the night before Angelica had arrived. She had been sneaking back to her house in the dark after visiting the horses when she had overheard her mom and dad talking on the patio. They were arguing quietly in the dark. Lisa stood frozen in her steps, listening. She couldn't risk moving forward or backward. A twig might crack underfoot or Neptune might bark at her and she would be discovered. So she held as still as she could in the shadows, grateful she had been creeping close to the big hydrangea when she had heard the voices. The bush was tall and thick and easy to hide behind.

"I promise you I'll get it back," her dad had suddenly burst out. Lisa's mom had said something in response, but her words were lost in the thump of footsteps walking across the patio. Lisa's dad stood right beside her, leaning onto the railing above her head and staring out into the darkness. Lisa shrunk back into the bush as far as she could, and held her breath.

"I promise you, Emily," Lisa's dad had said to her mom, "I will get our home back, and I don't really care how."

"It's just a house, Edward," said Lisa's mom.

"Just a house? Just a house?" Lisa's dad had roared. When Lisa's mom tried to shush him he only yelled louder. "How can you say that, Emily? It's been in my family for generations. It's the girls' inheritance. It's…it's my life!"

"Oh Edward, it's not your life," Lisa's mom had said quietly. Lisa could imagine her shaking her head. "There are so many things more important than a house. It's your pride that's been hurt. Not your life." When there was no reply, Lisa's mom walked closer to her husband, but then suddenly her steps had retreated and Lisa imagined that her dad had shrugged away her mom's embrace. Her mom's voice came again from the doorway, and Lisa could tell she was on the verge of tears. "You need to rethink what's important. Stone and brick and wood are not important. It's just a house, Edward. You need to open your eyes to what really matters." Then she firmly pulled the door shut behind her and silence had again pervaded the night.

Lisa's dad was silent for a long time. When her foot began to itch, she longed to shift her weight and reach into her shoe to scratch her heel, but she didn't dare move. Finally she heard his voice, low and calm and deadly serious. "I'll get it back," he said, his voice almost a growl. "I don't care what I have to do or how long it takes, I'll get it back even if I have to kill Pickering to get it."

Suddenly he had spun around, and Lisa heard his quick footsteps crossing the patio. He slammed the door behind him when he went inside their small house.

Moments later Lisa had slipped into her bedroom window, still shaking from the inconceivable words that had come from her father's mouth. She had tried to sleep for hours after that, but every time she had begun to drift off, the words forced their way back into her mind, "I'll get it back even if I have to kill Pickering to get it."

Why would Lisa not tell me what is troubling her? Is she protecting someone? Is she afraid to tell me? Only one thing is certain, she does not really believe it is nothing.

There is so much yet I cannot see. So much that the horses cannot tell me, because they do not know. How can I keep them safe if I do not understand what threatens them? How can I keep Lisa safe if she does not tell me what she fears?

I must watch and listen and learn. Quickly. Lisa's life may depend on it, as well as the lives of Jupiter and the others. Lisa and the horses are the truly innocent ones. I must protect them. But from whom? From where does the danger come?

It's finally time to do something about him, tonight around 10 p.m., if all goes according to plan. And it will. There aren't any holes in my plan. It's perfect. He's just waiting there for me, like a fly in my web. Finally, after all these years of waiting, satisfaction.

Lisa tried to phone Mr. Pickering when she got home and then again just before supper, but both times the phone just rang and rang. The second time she phoned, she let it ring more than 20 times before she hung up the receiver.

When supper was finished, Lisa cleared away the dishes and began her homework. She had so much to catch up on. By 8:30 p.m. she only had two pages of math questions left and an English assignment to do that she had been putting off. When her mom put Molly to bed at 9 p.m., she was almost finished her math homework. Lisa finished the last question as her mom walked back into the kitchen and began to empty the dishwasher. She leaned back in her chair and closed her eyes. *Now just my English assignment*, she thought. *And all I have to do is write a paragraph that describes a person's character.*

She could hear the gentle noise of her mom moving around the kitchen and putting the shining cups and plates away in the cupboards. The sound was comforting. Lisa sighed with her eyes still closed. Peaceful moments at home in the evenings were rare these days. Usually she ended up doing her homework in her bedroom so she wouldn't have to be around her dad. Even when he didn't say anything she could feel his anger. She pictured it like a dark swarm of bees buzzing around him, with one or two occasionally zipping out to sting someone in the family. But today was different. Her dad was gone. Her homework was almost completed. The horses had had a wonderful day. And Angelica was there to help take care of them.

"Mom," she said, opening her eyes and sitting up straight. "Who should I write about? I have to write a paragraph for English class that describes someone's appearance and the way I describe them has to tell about their personality." Lisa's mom put the last dish in the cupboard and sat in the chair across the table from Lisa. She pulled her feet up onto the chair and settled there, cross-legged.

"Write about me," she said and smiled with her small perfect teeth.

"Okay," said Lisa slowly. "Let me think of what to write." She looked closely at her mom's face, like a painter studying her subject. Her mom's eyes were large, her nose and chin small and pointy. *I wish I looked more like her and less like Dad,* thought Lisa as her mom yawned in her chair. While Lisa's eyes were almond-shaped and blue, her mom's and Molly's were round and a rich brown. Lisa's hair was dark blonde, long and thick, unlike the wispy reddish-brown curls that belonged to her mother. Lisa watched as her mom stretched gracefully in her chair. *Just like a cat,* thought Lisa. *While I always look so clumsy.*

"You look a lot like Molly," said Lisa.

"Poor kid," said Lisa's mom with a smile.

Lisa didn't argue with her mom or tell her she thought Molly was lucky. Her mom would have argued back, but Lisa knew the truth. Molly and her mom were the pretty ones in the family. *But I'm the artist,* she reminded herself. *And honestly, I think I'd rather be artistic than pretty. Especially after what Angelica said today about the down side of being beautiful. And besides, being artistic is a lot of fun.*

"I think I know what to write," said Lisa. "I can tell about your personality by comparing you to a cat."

"A cat!" exclaimed Lisa's mom, laughing.

"Yeah, you're pretty like a cat, and you stretch like a cat, and you move quietly like a cat. In fact, there are a lot of things about you that are catlike, Mom," said Lisa.

Lisa's mom smiled again. "So that's why cats are my favorite pet," she said. She fell silent as Lisa began to write, her pen skimming over the page. Every few seconds, Lisa would look up and search her mom's face as she tried to find the right descriptive word. When Lisa was almost finished, her mom spoke again. "Are you still going over to visit the horses?" she asked quietly.

For a moment, Lisa was taken back. While she didn't think her mom would be as unreasonable as her dad, she wasn't sure her mom wouldn't tell him. An uncomfortable silence swept into the kitchen.

"Okay, you don't have to tell me," Lisa's mom continued. "Just make sure you're always safe." She dropped her feet quietly to the floor and reached over the table to touch Lisa's hand. "Don't do anything risky, okay? Promise?"

Lisa looked up from her paper. "I wouldn't do anything stupid, Mom," she said. "Don't worry." She remembered trying to squeeze around Angelica in their hiding place, when Jimmy was pretending to beat Jupiter. *But next time I'll be more careful,* she decided. *I know how sneaky he can be now.*

Her mom smiled. "Thanks, honey," she whispered. Then her voice came louder. "Well, I'm off to read my book in bed."

"I'll just do my good copy," Lisa said, motioning to her English assignment. "Then I'm going to bed too. I'm tired."

"Good night then, sweetie," said Lisa's mom. She touched her daughter on the shoulder and walked toward the door, but abruptly she paused and turned around. "How is he?" she asked. "How is my Topper?"

Lisa's eyes searched her mom's face. *Does she want to know the truth,* she wondered, *or should I just tell her that they're fine? That would probably be the smartest thing. But how can I lie to my mom?*

She looked down at her hands. "He misses you. He doesn't understand what's happened. None of them do," she whispered. "They want us to come home." Silence followed her words and after a moment, Lisa looked up to see her mom fighting back tears, her eyes large and luminous. *Should I tell her about Jimmy?* she wondered. *Should I tell my mom how he's been mistreating them?*

Suddenly a car pulled into the driveway, the light from its headlights streaking across the wall. "Lets talk about this tomorrow," said Lisa's mom. "It looks like your dad's home. How odd. I thought he had a meeting in the city early tomorrow morning."

"Don't tell Dad I'm still going over there," pleaded Lisa. "Please Mom."

"I won't," said her mom, brushing her tears onto her sleeve. "I promise."

The first thing that Lisa noticed about her dad when he walked in the door was that he looked exhausted. Dark circles hovered under his eyes like black half moons, and the rest of his face was lined and pale. His mouth was drawn in a tight, tense line.

"Are you okay, sweetheart?" Lisa's mom asked him as he gulped down a glass of water at the kitchen sink. "I've never seen you look so tired."

"I had a hard day," he replied and tried to smile. Lisa turned away. His smile looked so fake, just skin stretched over teeth. That's all. He muttered something about his

64

meeting being cancelled and how all he wanted to do was go to bed, then left the room. Lisa drew in a big breath of relief when he was gone.

Lisa's mom stopped beside her before she followed him. "It'll be okay, Lisa," she said reassuringly. "We'll get through this tough time. That's another promise I'll make." She reached out to stroke Lisa's hair as if she was a kitten. "We'll all be okay." Then she followed her husband out of the room.

Left in the quiet kitchen, Lisa forced herself to concentrate on finishing the last of her homework and then organized her school books in a neat pile on the table. She turned out the light and hurried to her room halfway down the dark hallway. Once the door was shut, she felt a little better. She switched on the light and tried reading to pass the time until 11 p.m., but she kept thinking of her mom and dad. *Will we really be okay?* she wondered. *Can I believe my mom? How can she know?*

Lisa sighed and dropped the book on the bed. It was no use. She couldn't concentrate. Her eyes strayed to the clock. It was 10:40 p.m. *Dad's probably asleep and, even if Mom isn't, she knows I go visit the horses anyway now,* Lisa thought as she slipped a dark sweatshirt over her yellow T-shirt. Somewhere in the back of her mind, she knew her mom wouldn't want her to be wandering around in the middle of the night, and she knew her mom certainly wouldn't want Lisa visiting the horses if she knew how horrid Jimmy was. *But Angelica will be with me,* Lisa reasoned, stuffing the thought down. *That makes it safer.*

Lisa threw back her covers and pushed her pillow into the center of the mattress. Then she positioned a couple of stuffed animals beside the pillow and drew her quilt back over top. It looked almost exactly like someone was sleep-

65

ing under the blankets. She turned off the light switch and, in the darkness, walked to her window and quietly pushed it open.

The damp smells of the night flowed into the room, and Lisa took a deep breath. She swung a leg over the windowsill, sat on the ledge, and then swung the other leg over. Quietly, she lowered herself to the ground. Neptune came to greet her with a whine in his throat.

"Shhh," whispered Lisa as she bent to stroke the dog. After scratching him behind his ears, she turned back to the window and pushed it so that it was almost closed. Neptune followed her along the back of the house and watched silently at the end of his chain as she moved around the corner.

Soon Lisa was standing beside the road in front of the house. The road was deserted. Because she didn't know which way Angelica would be coming, she sat in the tall grass beside her driveway and waited. The moon hadn't risen yet, but the sky was beginning to brighten as it came closer and closer to the horizon. Stars glistened in the sky. Lisa lay in the grass and pillowed her head on her arms. The stars were so beautiful—countless as the sands on the seashore, going on and on forever. The hill that she and Molly had climbed that morning was dark against the sky, the moonglow coming from behind it edging it in a thin outline of light. She could hear a cricket nearby fiddling a melody on his back legs, but other than that, the night was hushed.

Then a shaving of light topped the hill. The moon was rising, huge against the horizon. Lisa watched as the shaving grew larger and rounder and fuller, and finally, the full moon topped over the hill. The moonlight changed everything to liquid silver. Lisa held up her hand, her fingers

66

spread. The glow streamed between them and fell onto the grass like pools of fluid light.

The world becomes magical under a moon like this one, thought Lisa. *It's as if anything could happen on a night like tonight. Anything. Maybe my mom is right. Maybe we will be okay.*

It's mine. It's finally mine. The Manor. The land. The money. No one can stop me now. All I have to do is find that new will and destroy it. And I will find it. No one knows it exists except me, and I can look for it while I sell off all the furniture and other stuff in the house. My uncle almost made this too easy. I didn't even have to carry him down to the stable as I planned. He went down all by himself before I got there.

But come to think of it, that bothers me. Why was he in the stable when I got back tonight? I know now I didn't give him enough of the drug to keep him unconscious, but why did he go to the stable instead of going for help? It's probably nothing, I know. But it bugs me. Maybe he just wanted to see the horses, to see if they were all right. Worrying about horses when he's the one in trouble…old fool! Or maybe, just maybe, he was trying to leave a message for that kid. I wonder if I should go back right now? Or stick to the plan and return later?

In the distance Lisa heard a car pull out of a driveway and tires squeal on pavement as it sped away. Then, in the silence that followed, she heard the whisper of footsteps on the road. Lisa lay still and listened as the feet turned into her driveway, barely crunching the gravel. She turned her head and watched as Angelica stopped in the driveway beside her. Angelica made no greeting, and Lisa wondered if the older girl had seen her hidden in the long grasses. She watched as Angelica took a deep breath, closed her eyes and raised her face to the night sky. Her golden hair rippled in the moonlight and her skin was as white as milk. Angelica stood still and allowed the moonlight to wash over her, just as Lisa had been doing only moments before.

"Hi," Lisa finally said. She sat up in the long grass.

If Angelica was surprised to see her beside the driveway, she didn't show it. "Hello," she said, opening her eyes and turning to Lisa. "Sorry to be late."

"You're not," said Lisa, climbing to her feet. "I think I'm early."

As they walked to Evergreen Manor, the two girls spoke little. Lisa told Angelica she hadn't been able to reach Mr. Pickering on the telephone and then let the peaceful silence surround them once more. The night was too glorious for mere speech. It inspired awe and hushed whispers, reflection and stillness, not words. *Just breathe the silver air*, thought Lisa. *Breathe beauty*. She knew that Angelica was probably waiting for her to talk about what had been bothering her. *But I just can't tell her. Not yet,* Lisa thought. *The night is too beautiful to ruin with ugly thoughts and words.*

The magic stayed with Lisa until they turned into the driveway at Evergreen Manor and she looked at the dark house. It squatted behind the paddocks like a giant black toad. Lisa felt tears spring to her eyes. The house looked so different now that Jimmy lived there, though nothing outwardly had really changed. It wasn't her home anymore. She was no longer welcome.

But it's even more than that, she thought. *It's more than just not homey. It's as if something dark lurks behind the shadows and stares at us now and, if we turn and look suddenly, trying to catch it, it's gone. It's as if there is something there, whispering terrible things to us we can almost hear. Mr. Pickering changed the house a bit, but not in a bad way. It was Jimmy. He's the one who really took my home away from me. Not Dad or Mr. Pickering. Jimmy's the one who made it seem evil.*

Her eyes searched for his car parked in its usual place in front of the Manor, but if he had returned, his car was out of sight in the garage. As her eyes roamed over the dark house, her face became puzzled. *Even if Jimmy's gone and Mr. Pickering is asleep, there still should be a light on somewhere,* she thought. *The house is too dark. Too quiet.*

"Something is wrong," said Angelica, her voice hushed.

"The lights are all out," said Lisa. Her throat tightened, and she felt the poisonous vapor of fear float higher and higher inside of her, shutting off her breathing. "The house is too dark."

"No. Not in the house. In the stable," said Angelica, her voice now loud in the stillness. "The horses are afraid. I can feel it!"

70

Lisa didn't hesitate to ask how Angelica knew. She just ran. She wasn't worried about being seen anymore. If there was something wrong with the horses, she didn't care if Jimmy was there, didn't care if he was hiding somewhere waiting for her. She had to get to the stable as fast as she could. She had to save them.

She glanced back once to see Angelica running swiftly and silently behind her. The moonlit stable grew larger in front of them as they ran. Then Lisa's hand was on the handle and the door was open. The stable interior gaped black and cavernous before her. The horses' fear rolled out and hit her like a wave. She could hear them thumping and pacing in their stalls as she fumbled for the light. She felt Angelica standing beside her.

"Jupiter," Angelica whispered. "It is Jupiter." When Lisa found the light switch, she saw Angelica already walking toward Jupiter's stall at the end of the stable row.

Jupiter neighed loudly when he saw them, calling them to him. "What's wrong?" cried Lisa as she ran toward him, passing Angelica. She tried to sound normal, but even she could hear the panic in her voice.

I've got to be calm for Jupiter, she told herself. *He'll be even more frightened if I panic. And there's nothing to be afraid of anyway. There's no one here. Everything looks fine.* She concentrated on stopping her hands from shaking as she leaned over the stall door to stroke his neck. She moved to the side as Angelica came up behind her, so she could help calm Jupiter. It was then she noticed the bundle of clothing lying on the straw inside Jupiter's stall.

"Angelica, look at this," she said. "Someone threw some old clothes into…" Suddenly a wall of terror slammed into her and she staggered backward. Angelica reached out and grabbed her before she fell.

71

"What is it, Lisa?" she asked, but Lisa couldn't speak. She couldn't tell Angelica about the thin hand that had been extruding from the dirty clothing. The gray mop of hair in disarray. She couldn't form the words. All she could do is point. Angelica led Lisa to the bale of straw Jimmy had beaten the day before and helped her sit down. Behind them, Jupiter's panicky neigh rang out again and his hoof hit the stall door with a loud bang.

"Lay your head down onto your knees," Angelica suggested. "That way the dizziness will pass. And breathe slowly. I will be right back."

With her head on her knees, Lisa watched Angelica's feet hurry toward Jupiter's stall. She raised her head when the older girl opened the stall door and then stood back to let Jupiter out of his enclosure. The black gelding leaped out of the stall and trotted stiff-legged past Lisa to the far end of the stable. Firefly neighed to him, and Lisa heard the clunk of his hooves as he went to stand beside her.

Lisa watched Angelica walk into the stall and then disappear as she knelt down. Like a sleepwalker, Lisa stood and walked to the stall door. Angelica was kneeling in the straw beside the still form lying face down in the straw. Lisa saw her reach out and touch the exposed wrist, then her hand moved to his neck. Finally she turned to Lisa.

"He is dead," Angelica said.

Poor, poor Mr. Pickering. Could I have saved him? Was there something I could have done, something the Great One would have allowed me to do? What Mr. Pickering's last hour must have been like, I can only imagine. He did not deserve this. And poor Lisa. She liked him so much. She recognized he was a lonely man and a good man.

Jupiter is going to be blamed. The police will assume he killed his owner. Is this why I was sent here? To save Jupiter from being destroyed? Or are he and Lisa and the others still in danger from the one who did this? I must ask Jupiter what happened, as soon as Lisa is safe at home.

Tears erupted from Lisa's eyes, instantly blinding her.

"He is Mr. Pickering, is he not?" asked Angelica.

Lisa could only nod in reply. She put her head down and buried her face in her hands. Sobs started to shake her shoulders. She felt Angelica's arms around her, leading her back to the bale of straw, then pulling her down to sit beside her. She felt Jupiter touch her shoulder with his muzzle and heard him nicker to her.

"It's my fault," the strangled words emerged from Lisa's throat.

"It is *not* your fault," said Angelica beside her. "You did nothing wrong."

"But you were right. We should have told someone he was sick," said Lisa, gasping. "I was so weak, afraid my dad would be too angry with me if I said anything. And I thought Jimmy wouldn't leave him if he was too sick. Why did he leave? Didn't he care that Mr. Pickering might die?"

"He did not die because he was sick, Lisa," said Angelica softly. Her voice sounded different, and Lisa looked up into her golden eyes.

"What do you mean?" asked Lisa, dumbfounded.

"He was killed," said Angelica.

"What?" said Lisa, not sure she had understood. "You mean someone murdered him?"

Solemnly Angelica nodded her head.

"But why? Who?" asked Lisa, her mind beginning to buzz.

"I do not know why. But who? Maybe …"

Angelica's mouth continued to move, but suddenly Lisa couldn't hear her anymore. Her head swelled with the words she had heard only two nights before. *I'll get it back even if I have to kill Pickering to get it.* All she could think of was her dad's pale face and sunken eyes when he walked in the door that night. She pictured him trying to smile, trying to convince her that everything was okay, that everything was normal.

Lisa felt a strange numbness begin to creep over her. It started at her lips, and spread slowly to her face and neck and arms. Nothing seemed real anymore. The stable was like a dream. She stared at the straw strewn floor, trying to think of anything other than Mr. Pickering lying dead in Jupiter's stall. Trying to imagine anyone but her dad leaning over him. Angelica sat beside her for a few moments and tried to get her to talk, but Lisa couldn't say a single word. She was afraid she would let everything spill out if she opened her mouth. *And I can't tell anyone,* she thought. *I can't let anyone know what he did. He's my dad. I have to protect him. He didn't know what he was doing.*

When Angelica stood, Lisa barely noticed. "I am going to telephone the police," she said and touched Lisa's arm. "Will you be okay here or do you want to come with me?" she asked.

Lisa barely shook her head. "I'll stay. I have Jupiter with me. Can you call my mom too?" she asked in a small voice.

"Of course," said Angelica and began to walk toward the door to the stable. Just before leaving, she turned back. "Umm, Lisa?" she said, her voice unsure for the first time. "I cannot be here when the police come. Please, do not tell them about me, okay?"

Lisa looked up puzzled and then climbed to her feet. She

turned toward Jupiter, leaned her cheek on his lowered face and looked at Angelica with red eyes. "Why not?" she asked.

"I cannot tell you why now. You and Jupiter need help and there is no time. But trust me, okay?" said Angelica. Her amber eyes pleaded with Lisa.

Lisa was silent for a moment and then she nodded her head. She would keep Angelica's secret too, whatever it was. She watched as Angelica slipped out the stable door into the night.

The moment she was gone, Lisa pulled away from Jupiter. She gathered her courage and stepped toward the stall. *I only have a few minutes,* she thought. *If there is anything here that shows my dad did this, I've got to find it now.*

When she saw Mr. Pickering's body, so thin and frail in the straw, the tears sprung to her eyes again. *I'm so sorry,* she thought as she knelt in the straw beside him. "I'm so sorry my dad did this to you," she whispered. "And I'm sorry I'm trying to hide what he did. He just loved this place too much. You loved it too. You told me, remember? On that day we had the picnic."

Lisa remembered the day vividly. It was a sunny summer afternoon just three weeks before Jimmy had come to stay with Mr. Pickering. Mr. Pickering had made a picnic lunch for her and they had eaten it in one of the horse paddocks, the one with the big maple tree. Dakota kept trying to steal the buns, and Mr. Pickering had laughed until he had had tears in his eyes. Then he had told Lisa he had worked at Evergreen Manor as a boy. His father had been the head groom and his young son, not called Mr. Pickering then but Charlie, had loved working with the horses and helping his dad. He told her it had been the happiest time of his life. His family had fallen on hard times shortly after they left

77

Evergreen Manor and, for the rest of his life, Mr. Pickering had wanted to return. When he heard the Manor was up for sale, he could hardly believe his luck and had sold almost everything he owned so he could buy it.

Lisa remembered vividly the look in his eyes when he told her he was sorry for taking her home away from her. She had smiled and told him she was just glad she could still see Jupiter, but he could tell her smile was sad. He had leaned back against the tree and the two of them watched the horses in silence. When they began to pack up their picnic leftovers, he had promised Lisa he would never sell the horses and told her again that she was always welcome at Evergreen Manor.

Lisa reached out and put her hand in the pocket of Mr. Pickering's robe. It was empty. Quickly she stood and glanced toward the door. There was still no sign of Angelica. She stepped to the other side of Mr. Pickering and tried to check the other pocket. It was partially beneath his body, and she pulled on the material. She could hear sirens in the distance coming closer and closer. *The police,* thought Lisa, *I need to hurry.*

She gave the material a sharp tug to free the pocket and Mr. Pickering's arm slid toward her. Lisa jumped backward and fell into the straw, her fear instantly rising around her, blocking her breathing and roaring in her ears. She stared in horror at the dark bruises blooming over Mr. Pickering's exposed arm like black flowers and then, mercifully, tears clouded her vision again. Through the blur, Lisa noticed something white in Mr. Pickering's hand. She reached out and gingerly pulled the piece of paper from his stiff fingers then, holding her breath, she checked his other robe pocket. Nothing again. She slipped the piece of paper into her jeans pocket as she stood and moved away from the body.

"I'm sorry," she whispered as she backed toward the door. "I'm sorry this wasn't the perfect place you thought it was, Mr. Pickering. You have no idea how much I wish it had been."

Suddenly, Lisa heard someone run up behind her. As she began to turn around, a firm hand fell onto her shoulder, rooting her in place. Then her dad's voice boomed out. "Why are you here, Lisa? What have you done?"

Slowly Lisa turned toward her father, but no words came out of her mouth. His face looked even more haggard than before and a strange light was in his eyes. Without meaning to, she pulled from his grasp and stepped away from him.

"Are you okay?" her dad asked, his voice cracking with emotion. Lisa stared at him, her eyes filled with fear. Slowly she nodded, though she didn't feel okay at all. She felt worse than she had ever felt in her life, but how could she tell him the horrible accusations that were running through her head.

Mr. Pickering worked his whole life just to save enough money to return to a place where he remembered being happy, she thought. *If my dad killed him, he must be a monster. But how can I condemn him? It's my fault too. I helped to kill Mr. Pickering by not letting anyone know what my dad said. And by becoming Mr. Pickering's friend. If I hadn't done that, Dad wouldn't have hated him so much.*

Lisa watched her dad's eyes move to the body lying in the straw inside Jupiter's stall. She was surprised to see sadness and pity crawl onto his face and then the sirens were right outside the stable. Lisa could see the lights flashing through the darkness outside the open door, scattering the moonlight into oblivion. Within seconds, the police burst into the stable.

Lisa watched as the mask closed over her father's face and he became professional and businesslike, emotionless.

She shut her eyes and tried to remember his exact expression from moments before. She had seen compassion on his face, hadn't she? Hadn't he looked sorry for Mr. Pickering? But the expression had disappeared so quickly, she just wasn't sure. She slipped her hand into her pocket and clutched at the slip of paper she had picked from Mr. Pickering's fingers.

A loud thud caught her attention, and she turned around. Jupiter was standing with his head in Firefly's stall and his back to the officers, rolling his eyes. Lisa could see he was terrified. Being locked in a stall with Mr. Pickering had taken its toll and now, with all the strangers in the stable, Jupiter was becoming frightened beyond reason.

"Wait," she called to a policewoman who was approaching Jupiter with a halter in her hand. "Let me do it. He knows me." Jupiter's front hoof flashed out and struck the door of Firefly's stall again, sending the sound ricocheting through the stable.

Lisa hurried to his side. "It's okay, Jupie," she said. "I'll take you outside so you can run in the paddock a bit, okay?" She reached out and took the halter the policewoman held toward her and slipped it over Jupiter's head.

"Just hold him there for a few minutes, will you?" said another officer, as he approached. "Will he let us examine him?"

"As long as I hold him, he will," said Lisa. "But he's very frightened." More people walked into the stable and the officer called one of the women over.

"I'm Inspector Frederick," he introduced himself to Lisa. "And this is Dr. Callick, one of our forensic specialists. She'll need to examine the horse before we turn him out."

"Why?" asked Lisa suspiciously.

"The body is in the stall that this horse came out of, isn't

81

it?" asked Dr. Callick as she slid her hand over Jupiter's neck.

"Yes," said Lisa slowly. Then suddenly she understood. "You think he killed Mr. Pickering?" she asked incredulously. "Jupiter wouldn't hurt anyone, especially Mr. Pickering. He liked Mr. Pickering."

Dr. Callick ran her hand down Jupiter's front leg and asked him to pick up his hoof. Jupiter tossed his head as he raised his foreleg. Lisa could tell he didn't like Dr. Callick very much, probably because he could sense she didn't like him. "You don't understand," Lisa tried again. "There is absolutely no way Jupiter would attack Mr. Pickering, I swear."

Dr. Callick took some dirt samples from Jupiter's hoof, then pared away a little from the hoof itself. Lisa noticed the part she pared away had a dark spot on it. "That isn't blood on his hoof," she said defensively.

"Please," said Dr. Callick, putting Jupiter's hoof down and turning to Lisa. "If you are so sure he didn't do it, then there's nothing to worry about, is there? The tests will only prove he is innocent." She moved around to Jupiter's off side, took samples from his other front hoof and put them into another neatly labelled container. Then she took samples from Jupiter's back hooves.

When she was finished, Dr. Callick went back to Jupiter's head. She reached up to stroke Jupiter's neck. He rolled his eyes at her and her hand froze in midair. Then she lowered it to his muzzle so he could sniff at her. Jupiter inhaled her scent, his eyes on her face. "He's very frightened, isn't he? It must have been hard for him, locked in the stall with his owner dead," she said. She glanced toward the police officers standing with Lisa's dad and Mr. Pickering's body, then leaned toward Lisa. "Try not to worry. I know horses and, you're right, he doesn't act like a killer."

"Thanks," whispered Lisa. The unexpected kindness made her want to cry again. She blinked her tears back and leaned on Jupiter's neck.

"You can turn him out now if you want," suggested Dr. Callick and patted her on the shoulder. "He looks like he could use the peace and quiet for a while. And like I said, don't worry. Everything will be okay."

I've heard that so many times tonight, thought Lisa. *Everything is not okay! Mr. Pickering has been killed, maybe by my own father, Jupiter may be blamed for it and Angelica left me here to face it all alone. How is that okay?*

"Come on, Jupie," she said aloud and began to lead him toward the stable door. Inspector Frederick saw her begin to leave and left the group standing around the body. "Wait, Lisa," he called after her. "I don't want you to take him out alone."

"You're right. He should have company," said Lisa, though she knew Inspector Frederick meant he was afraid Jupiter would attack her too. "I'll take Topper out with him."

She turned back to Topper's stall and grabbed his halter hanging on the hook outside the stall door. She slipped inside the stall, leaving Jupiter's lead rope hanging over the door and put the halter on the gray gelding's head. "Good boy, Topper," she murmured when the halter was in place. "You get to go outside tonight, you lucky boy." Lisa picked up Jupiter's lead rope and led the two horses toward Inspector Frederick standing at the stable door.

"You can take Topper," she said to the Inspector, holding the gray's lead rope out to him. Then she walked outside with Jupiter. The same magical moon glowed in the sky, and Lisa stopped to look up at it. Jupiter nickered to her and nuzzled her back.

Suddenly, Lisa thought of leaping onto Jupiter's back and galloping away. Away from Mr. Pickering's body lying in the straw—away from her dad and the police, and their accusing eyes. Away from the home that wasn't her home anymore. Just ride and ride and ride in the moonlight, and never come back. She twisted her fingers in Jupiter's mane. It would only take a second to vault onto his back and, thanks to Angelica, she already knew how to ride him without a saddle or bridle. The Inspector wouldn't be able to stop her. They would be gone almost before he would realize it, fading into the night, never to return.

Unconsciously, her hand slipped into her pocket and touched the slip of paper. She had only gotten a glimpse of it, but she knew it was a car rental slip. She had seen them before at home: slips from the same company that her dad usually rented from when he needed a car in the city and had to leave the family car for her mom to use.

How could she leave her dad? Maybe he needed her help still. And her mom and Molly, how could she leave them? And Neptune, Topper, Firefly, and Dakota? They all needed her, especially now that Mr. Pickering had been killed. Lisa hung her head. There was no escape. There would be no riding off in the moonlight. She had to stay. There was no choice. *I'll have to trust that Dr. Callick is right,* she thought. *I'll have to trust that they can prove Jupiter's innocence.*

She opened the gate to the front paddock and led Jupiter through. Inspector Frederick led Topper in behind her. Silently, Lisa slipped Jupiter's halter from his head, and then showed Inspector Frederick how to undo the buckle and let Topper free. The two horses wandered slowly away, picking at the autumn grass as Lisa closed and latched the gate behind them. As she walked beside the Inspector back

84

to the stable she looked over her shoulder one last time. Topper was a silver horse in the moonlight and Jupiter a dark shadow beside him. They were walking toward the other side of the paddock and looked relaxed and calm.

Then Lisa saw something else: a glimmer of gold rippling in the soft light on the other side of the paddock. Angelica. Lisa turned quickly away. She didn't want Inspector Frederick to look in Angelica's direction. A small smile played on her lips. *So she didn't abandon me. I'm so glad she's here,* thought Lisa. *She'll take care of Jupiter while I talk to the police.*

Back in the stable, Inspector Frederick asked Lisa to sit on the bale of straw and wait. He had some questions for her, but needed to do a few things first. Lisa watched and listened to the police officers as they investigated the crime scene. They looked at everything in Jupiter's stall, even searching through the straw and checking the floor underneath. Then they began to examine the rest of the stable. The police photographer took pictures of everything. Then Inspector Frederick began to ask her questions.

Lisa was glad the police didn't seem to realize that her dad was involved yet. They asked her what she had seen, about Mr. Pickering's illness and Jimmy, and about the horses. She had a hard time making everything sound as if Angelica hadn't been there and, when the questions finally were finished, she hoped she hadn't said anything to make the police suspicious toward her dad either. There had been so many questions. Some of them didn't even seem to relate to Mr. Pickering being murdered, and Lisa didn't know why the police were asking them. Her dad sat beside her the whole time and, once when Lisa had felt overcome by sadness, he asked the police to stop until Lisa felt she was ready to continue.

When it was over, Lisa's dad led her to his car. Lisa sat stiffly on her side of the front seat as they drove home. She kept expecting him to say something about how Mr. Pickering deserved what he got or to be angry with her for sneaking out, but he was quiet the entire way home. When they pulled into the driveway, Lisa was relieved to see the kitchen lights on and her mom standing at the window. As soon as the car stopped, Lisa opened the door. She was about to escape when her dad caught her arm. Lisa couldn't stop herself from gasping in fear.

"Are you okay, Lisa?" he asked.

She could hear the exhaustion in his voice and the lights from the house illuminated the bags under his eyes. She nodded, too afraid to say anything.

He looked at her with a puzzled expression as if trying to understand what was frightening her so much, then he let go of her arm. "You need some rest," he said. "And so do I. We'll talk tomorrow."

In the house, Lisa's mom hugged her. She had prepared a warm glass of milk for her daughter, and she walked to Lisa's bedroom with her.

"Do you want to talk about what happened?" she asked Lisa quietly, as she pulled the window shut and latched it. She moved to the bed and took Lisa's stuffed animals and pillow from under the covers.

"Maybe tomorrow," said Lisa, listlessly. "But I don't know for sure." She felt so tired, she wasn't even worried that her mom saw how she had snuck out.

"Okay honey," her mom said and. when Lisa's bed was made, she kissed her on the forehead just like she had done every night when Lisa was younger. "Don't worry about school. I'll call them in the morning and tell them you won't be in until Tuesday."

"Thanks Mom," whispered Lisa. As soon as her mother left the room, Lisa undressed and slipped into bed. She took a sip of the warm milk and laid back. She was so tired. Her entire mind and body seemed to ache with fatigue. But she couldn't sleep. Questions nagged at her, questions the police hadn't asked. She stared at the dark ceiling with aching eyes.

One of the things I don't understand is why Dad would want to frame Jupiter? she thought. *I know he likes Jupie. He helped me save him when he was an orphaned foal. And it's not just Jupie—I don't think Dad would blame Mr. Pickering's murder on any of the horses. He liked all of them and, no matter how angry he was at Mr. Pickering, he still wouldn't want any of them to be hurt. He would have thought of another plan.*

Lisa rolled over in bed and pulled the pillow over her head. She squeezed her eyes shut, but it didn't make her any sleepier. The thoughts continued. *And why did Angelica ask me to not tell the police she was there? Could she be involved in Mr. Pickering's murder somehow?*

Finally her thoughts turned to the man she had become fast friends with. *I am going to miss him so much,* she thought. *He was such a nice old man. And he just wanted to be happy. He was the best owner Evergreen Manor and the horses could have if we couldn't be there. How could Dad hate him so much? I don't understand.*

Suddenly, she gasped and sat upright. She turned on the lamp by her bed and hurried to where her jeans were laying in an untidy heap on the floor. The piece of paper was still in her pocket. She pulled it out and uncrumpled it. It was a car rental slip, just like she thought. But the renter's name on the slip was unfamiliar.

Thomas J. Short. Who is Thomas J. Short? thought Lisa. *Could my dad have used a fake name to rent the car? Or maybe, just maybe, someone else killed Mr. Pickering. That would make more sense than my dad. But who else would want Mr. Pickering dead? I can't imagine he would have any enemies.*

There was a light tapping at the window and Lisa spun toward the sound, her nerves raw. A dark form was silhouetted on the other side of the glass, the moon edging the golden hair in glowing light.

Cautiously, Lisa walked toward the window. She unlatched it and pushed it open just a bit, still keeping her hand on the latch so she could pull it shut in a hurry if she wanted to.

"You have to come with me," whispered Angelica. "We have to find out why Mr. Pickering was murdered."

"First tell me why you didn't want me to tell the police about you?" Lisa said to Angelica in a low voice.

"Did you tell them?" asked Angelica.

"No."

"I cannot tell you the whole reason why," Angelica said. "But I can tell you some of it. Come outside where we can easily talk."

Lisa looked suspiciously at Angelica. *Jupiter trusts her*, she remembered. *But does that mean I can trust her?* Finally she agreed. "Just give me a minute to get dressed again," she said. "I'll meet you in the driveway at the front of the house."

Angelica gave a little nod and moved quietly away from the window. Lisa turned back to her room and found her clothes where she had thrown them. She shoved the car rental slip back into her jeans pocket before she slipped them on. Soon she was dressed and ready to go. Neptune was lying near his doghouse in the back yard and Lisa stopped for a minute to scratch his ears, then she moved on.

Angelica was waiting for her in the driveway. "Okay, why didn't you want me to tell the police about you?" asked Lisa, not wasting any time. "Who are you, really? A criminal? Is that why you didn't want me to say anything?"

"No," said Angelica and sat down in the long grass at the edge of the driveway. She motioned to Lisa to sit beside her, but Lisa continued to stand. She wanted to hear Angelica's answer first. Angelica cleared her throat. "I am not what I seem," she said. "I am not a normal teenaged girl."

"No kidding," said Lisa, her voice hard.

Angelica didn't change her expression or react to Lisa's sarcasm. "But I am not a criminal. What I mean is that I understand horses," said Angelica. "I understand what they say and how they feel, and they can understand me too. Sometimes I can hear them calling me from far away."

"Yeah right. And I bet Jupiter or one of the other horses called you here," said Lisa, her voice full of disbelief.

"Yes, he did," said Angelica quietly. "I know it is hard to believe, but it is true. I felt his fear and came to help him."

"So, what are you, the patron saint for horses?" asked Lisa, her tone still sceptical.

"I know it sounds strange," Angelica admitted. "And honestly, it does not matter if you believe that part or not. I just hope you believe that I did not harm Mr. Pickering. Do you?"

"Why shouldn't I?" said Lisa. "You didn't want me to tell the police about you. What else am I supposed to think? I don't know anything about you. I don't even know where you live."

"I did not kill him. I promise I was not even there," Angelica said and lowered her head. She stared at her hands in her lap. "I wish I had been and maybe I could have saved him." When she looked up, Lisa noticed tears glinting in her eyes. "I asked you not to tell the police because they would not have believed I am innocent. You do not even believe me. They would have thought I knew something about the murder and would have wasted precious time asking me questions." She stopped speaking and Lisa could hear a night bird singing far away, its song true and clear. "Do you really think I killed him?" Angelica finally asked.

"No," said Lisa. "Jupiter walked toward you in the pasture when I turned him out tonight and that means he still trusts you. He wouldn't if he saw you murder Mr. Pickering." She walked to the side of the driveway and sat in the grass beside Angelica.

Angelica breathed a sigh of relief. "I am so glad you listen to Jupiter. A lot of owners do not listen to their horses."

"He's a good judge of character," said Lisa. "He loves everyone in my family, he learned to like Mr. Pickering and he's terrified of Jimmy."

"We should go back to the Manor," said Angelica. "We have to find out why Mr. Pickering was murdered, before it is too late."

"What do you mean?" asked Lisa.

"The horses are not out of danger yet. I cannot explain how I know or tell you what that danger is, but I can feel it," said Angelica. "There are things that have happened that do not make sense. If we can understand why they happened, we may understand why Mr. Pickering was murdered. And that can help us understand why the horses are still in danger." She climbed to her feet and held a hand out. Lisa didn't hesitate to take her hand but her face was creased in thought. She let Angelica pull her to her feet. "What are you thinking?" asked Angelica.

"It's nothing," Lisa replied after a moment. Though she didn't think Angelica had anything to do with Mr. Pickering's death, she still didn't want to tell her about the car rental slip. Not until she had more information. Not until she knew who had rented the car. "I'm just worried about the horses," she added.

"Me too," said Angelica as the two girls began to walk toward the Manor. "We have to investigate quickly. The biggest mystery to me is why Mr. Pickering was in the stable when the murderer found him."

"How do you know he wasn't forced out to the stable by the murderer?" asked Lisa.

"The front door to the Manor was open when I went to use the telephone, which, incidentally, was not working. I had to run to a payphone," said Angelica. "But I believe Mr. Pickering was so weak he did not think to shut the door when he left the house."

"Maybe he wanted to see if we had taken care of the horses," suggested Lisa.

"It could be that, yes," said Angelica. "But if Jimmy was not at the Manor, would he not trust you to take care of them?"

"Maybe he was going to ride to the hospital," suggested Lisa.

"But then would he not drive in his car?" asked Angelica. "It would be easier and faster than riding one of the horses."

"But what else could it be?" said Lisa, puzzled. "Unless…"

"Unless what?" asked Angelica, looking sharply at Lisa as they walked into the driveway of the Manor.

"The cubby hole," said Lisa. "Maybe he wanted to leave something in the cubby hole. It's a secret compartment behind a hidden door in Firefly's stall. You would never guess it was there even if you were looking right at it. It looks just like the wall in her stall."

"That could be it," said Angelica hopefully. "Maybe he wanted to leave something in there for you."

"He used to do that all the time," said Lisa wistfully, as they climbed through the fence to cut across the pasture. "If he knew I was going to be late getting to the stable, he would leave a snack for me. Sometimes he left me things as gifts. Once he left me a teacup and saucer that was from his grandma's favorite tea set. It was really pretty and had birch trees and spring flowers painted on it. He left an elephant figurine once too. My great-uncle brought it back from India years and years ago and, somehow, we had forgotten it in the house when we moved." Her voice was sad.

"You have missed your home a lot," said Angelica. She put her hand on Lisa's shoulder for a second. Lisa only nodded. *I miss Mr. Pickering even more,* she thought. She felt tears welling up inside of her and knew if she talked about him she would cry. With relief, she noticed Jupiter and Topper standing side by side beneath one of the trees in the paddock. They nickered to Lisa and Angelica as the girls approached.

"How're you doing, Jupie?" whispered Lisa. "Don't you worry. We're going to take care of everything." Then she turned to Angelica. "You say you can talk to horses?" she asked shyly. "Is he still frightened?"

Angelica smiled. "They are both still a bit on edge, but they are no longer frightened. They feel a lot better being away from the stable."

"Can you tell him that no matter what, I'll always take care of him?" asked Lisa.

Angelica nodded and turned to Jupiter. She put her hand behind his ear. Jupiter leaned down as Angelica began to whisper. Lisa listened as closely as she could but all she could hear was the wind brushing through the trees, a sigh softer than a whisper. Then Jupiter nickered and nuzzled Lisa. "He is saying thanks," said Angelica softly.

Lisa felt tears come to her eyes again. She loved Jupiter so much. *If it's the last thing I do, I'm going to keep him safe,* she vowed. *I'm not going to let him be blamed for Mr. Pickering's death. I'm not going to let Jimmy sell him to anyone but me. I don't care what it takes.*

She leaned onto Jupiter's forehead and stroked his neck for a moment. Then she pulled away. They had work to do. "I'll be back in a few minutes, Jupie," she said. "Don't you worry. Everything will be okay. I promise."

I was right to come back. That kid knows where it is, and she's going to get it tonight. All I have to do is follow along, far enough behind that they don't know I'm here.

I wonder who her friend is? She's beautiful! I would hate having to get rid of her too. But I have no choice. And it'll be just as easy to shut up two as it is one, at least the way I plan to do it.

I hate waiting! I hate this sneaking around! But I've got to stay cool long enough for them to lead me to the hiding place.

He is near. I can feel his presence but cannot tell where he is. Is he waiting for us in the stable? Is he watching us now? I can feel his impatience and know that he is waiting, but he is waiting for us to...to do what? I do not know yet. I must stay alert, no matter what. I must be ready for his attack and stop him from destroying the horses and Lisa. Because that is what he wants to do. I can feel it. I must stop him, at all costs. Even if I must sacrifice myself to do it.

Within moments Lisa and Angelica were approaching the stable. Lisa was just reaching to open the door, when Angelica put out her hand to stop her.

"What?" whispered Lisa, pulling her hand back. "What is it?"

"Let me go first," whispered Angelica. "Just stand next to the doorway against the wall until I call you, okay? If I do not call after two minutes or if you can tell something is wrong, run home and get your father."

"My dad?" whispered Lisa as she flattened herself next to the stable door. "Why my dad?"

"He is strong and he will find out what's happening here," replied Angelica.

"But I can't leave you," protested Lisa.

"Yes you can," replied Angelica. "You will have to if you want to save the horses." She unlatched the door and pushed it open. The tall black rectangle yawned before them. Lisa held her breath as Angelica slipped inside. Slowly she counted to 60 in her head. *Just one more minute Angelica. Please hurry.* Lisa strained to hear any noise she could, but the stable was silent. Even Firefly and Dakota were still. Lisa started to count to 60 again.

At the count of 45, Angelica poked her head out the stable door. "It is safe. Come inside," she said. "I will turn the light on after the door is shut in case he is watching us." Lisa ducked under the yellow tape that the police had strung across the doorway and stepped into the darkness. Angelica shut the door behind her and then light flooded the stable.

"Show me the cubby hole," said Angelica, as she started to walk toward Firefly's stall.

"Wait," said Lisa. Her words pulled Angelica to a stop. "You said 'he.' Who do you think is watching us?"

"Jimmy," said Angelica, then her eyes began to search Lisa's face. "You did not know he is the murderer?"

"Why do you think he's the murderer?" Lisa said, her voice breathless. "I thought he was the one who was keeping Mr. Pickering safe. I know they fought sometimes, but he's Mr. Pickering's nephew. He was taking care of him." Suddenly Lisa's knees felt weak. *My dad didn't do it,* the thought raced through her head. *My dad didn't do it!*

"Are you okay?" asked Angelica, her golden eyes filled with concern.

Lisa smiled weakly. "I thought my dad might have done it," she finally confessed. Now that she knew her father was innocent, the words came easily. Lisa could hear the relief in her voice as she spoke. "I heard him talking to my mom one night when I was sneaking home, and he was so angry. He said he was going to get Evergreen Manor back no matter what he had to do to get it, even if he had to kill Mr. Pickering. And I thought he meant it."

"Your dad may have been angry for having to sell your home, Lisa," said Angelica, softly. "But he is not a killer. Jimmy is. And Jupiter is the witness that told me."

"And Jimmy is here? Now?" asked Lisa.

"He is near," said Angelica. "I do not want to scare you, but we do not have very much time to find why he has returned or to stop him before he tries to harm us or the horses."

"Let's look in the cubby hole," said Lisa and started toward Firefly's stall again. "I just hope that's why Mr. Pickering came down to the stable tonight."

"And let us hope that Jimmy did not know the cubby hole was there," said Angelica as she opened the stall door and put her arms around Firefly's neck. She held the curious mare as Lisa walked into the stall and knelt beside the wall. She pushed in on one board and magically, a small door opened in front of her, revealing an opening the size of a small box.

"There's something here," said Lisa, her voice shaking. She picked up the crumpled paper lying on the bottom of the secret cupboard and spread it open on her lap. "It's a letter. But there's only a few words."

"What does it say?" asked Angelica.

"The writing is so shaky, I can't read it very well," said Lisa. She squinted with concentration, her nose almost touching the paper. "H-E something. It kind of drags across the page. The next word is easier. 'Dragged.'" She looked up. "What does 'dragged' have to do with anything?" she asked with a puzzled expression and then turned back to the writing.

"What is next?" asked Angelica. "Maybe it will help us figure out what the first two words mean."

"It's 'Jimmy,'" said Lisa. "Then it says something I can't read at all. It's three words, I think. The last one looks like 'hole.'"

"May I see?" asked Angelica. "Maybe I can understand."

Lisa stood and handed the paper to Angelica. She absent-mindedly stroked Firefly's neck as she peered at the paper Angelica held in front of them. "Hey, I know," Lisa suddenly said in an excited voice. "It says 'in Priest hole.' There's a Priest's Hole in our house. A long, long time ago when priests were being banned from their homeland, some rich Catholics put secret rooms in their houses to hide them from the army. The rooms had to be like the cubby hole, totally hidden from the outside. Mr. Pickering knew about the one

at Evergreen Manor only because I showed him how to get in, but no one else except our family knows about it."

"Jimmy does not know of it?" asked Angelica.

"Not unless Mr. Pickering told him about it," said Lisa. "I heard my dad say once that it's not even on any of the architectural drawings of the house. It's completely hidden."

Angelica held the paper up in front of them again. "And that word cannot be 'Dragged.' It does not make sense. It must be 'Drugged.'"

"Oh Angelica," said Lisa, her face suddenly growing pale. "Does that mean Mr. Pickering wasn't really sick? Jimmy was drugging him? If that's true, it means I could have saved him. I could have saved Mr. Pickering, if I had just seen what Jimmy was doing."

"How could you have seen it, Lisa?" asked Angelica firmly, turning to her and looking at her with compassionate eyes. "Do you know what someone looks and acts like when they are drugged? You knew Mr. Pickering was in bed a lot, so you thought he was sick. That is the logical conclusion to make. You must not blame yourself."

Lisa was silent for a moment as she tried to hold back her tears. Finally she raised her eyes to Angelica and nodded. "I'll try not to," she said quietly, though she didn't know *how* not to.

Angelica put her hand on Lisa's shoulder. "It will get easier with time," she added.

"So when Jimmy left yesterday morning, he didn't give Mr. Pickering enough of the drug to keep him asleep all day," said Lisa, forcing herself to get back to the matter at hand.

"And the 'H-E-something' word? Could it be 'help'?" asked Angelica.

"Help! Yes. He was asking for help. He left this note in the cubby hole, because he wanted me to get help for him," said

Lisa. "Jimmy had left him alone all day and the drug must have been wearing off, so he had enough presence of mind to come down to the stable to leave a note while he could."

"He probably knew he would not be able to escape by himself," continued Angelica. "He was too weak to drive to safely, and he could not use the phone because Jimmy disconnected it."

"And when Jimmy came back to murder him…" Lisa began, then her voice faded away. She couldn't say the rest of the words.

"He found him in the stable instead of in his bed," continued Angelica softly. "Mr. Pickering must have been too weak to go back to his bedroom."

"It's so horrible," whispered Lisa. "And I still don't understand why he did it. Why would he want to kill his own uncle? It doesn't make sense. Jimmy was probably going to inherit the Manor from Mr. Pickering, so he could have lived here for as long as he liked. And Mr. Pickering wasn't selfish or stingy. He would have given Jimmy whatever he wanted," she added sadly.

"Maybe Jimmy was in a hurry to get his inheritance," suggested Angelica.

"But why wouldn't he just live here and wait? Even if he didn't care about his uncle, he would still be taking a big chance on being caught."

Angelica shook her head. "I know," she said. "Some humans just do not make any sense. He had everything in his hands, and he threw it all away."

"There's got to be more to this than just Jimmy getting in a hurry for his inheritance," said Lisa. "Lets go check out the Priest's Hole. We've got to find what Mr. Pickering left there for me. We've got to find out why he was murdered."

Lisa and Angelica quickly left the stable in darkness behind them. They moved around to the front of the Manor keeping in the shadows of the trees and shrubs as much as possible. The moonlight was as bright as ever. Lisa and Angelica peered into the windows of the Manor as they hurried past, but the rooms were deserted.

If only I had stayed and watched through the window for a few extra minutes last night, thought Lisa. *I could have seen what was going on and gone for help. This is all my fault. I've got to find out why Mr. Pickering was murdered. I owe him that, at least.*

"Jimmy was looking for something hidden in the books," said Angelica. "Probably the same thing we hope to find in the Priest's Hole. We need to hurry."

"First, we have to find the keys to one of the secret doors," Lisa whispered to Angelica. "My great grandfather added locks to the Priest's Hole because my grandpa kept sneaking in there when he was a little boy. Once he fell down the stairs inside the Priest's Hole and broke his arm so his dad had a special locksmith come in and make keys for the two doors. The keys look like figurines, horse figurines, one black and the other one white. The black key is for the secret door in the sitting room and the white key is for the upstairs door."

"Where do you think the figurines will be?"

"I'm not sure. I wish Mr. Pickering had left them in the

cubby hole too," replied Lisa as they approached the front door. "But there's no reason to hide them because Jimmy could look right at them and not know what they were. I'm guessing they will be in the rooms where the two secret doors are."

"I hope Jimmy did not break them when he was searching the house," said Angelica.

"Me too," agreed Lisa. She paused at the front door and took a deep breath. "Do you think Jimmy could be inside?"

"It is possible," said Angelica. "But unlikely. We have to risk it."

Lisa turned the knob and then pulled back as the un-locked door swung open. The entrance hall was pitch black. "I wish we had a flashlight," Lisa whispered.

"I can see a bit," said Angelica. "Just stay close to me. You will have to tell me which room to go into however, as I do not know the house."

"The sitting room is through the second door on your left," whispered Lisa behind her. Angelica moved forward into the darkness, her hand trailing along the wall, with Lisa close behind her. After a few moments, Lisa's eyes began to adjust to the darkness, and she was surprised at how much she could see too. The first doorway to their left was closed, but the second was standing open. Lisa felt a rush of fear jolt through her as she followed Angelica into the black room.

"Close the door," whispered Angelica. Lisa quietly closed the door behind them and then watched Angelica's dark form move against the moonlit night as she hurried from window to window, closing the heavy draperies. "Now we can turn on a light," said Angelica.

Lisa moved toward a lamp she remembered Mr. Pickering had put on an end table, tripped over one of the couch cushions lying on the floor and bumped her shin on the coffee table in front of the sofa. She bit back her words as the pain peaked and finally began to fade. *That will be a big bruise tomorrow,* she thought as she made her way to the lamp. Then she switched on the light. The lamp was tiny and left the edges of the room in shadow.

Quickly, Angelica and Lisa began to search for the figurine. Some of the ornaments were scattered across the floor, a few of them in pieces. Angelica picked up one of a black horse. "Is this it?" she asked excitedly, her golden hair flowing around her shoulders.

"It could be. Let's see," said Lisa as she moved closer and reached out to take the figurine. "That's it! Good thing it wasn't broken," she said, taking it in her hand. "Come on, I'll show you how it works." Lisa led Angelica toward the fireplace. "Look at the bottom of the figurine," she said once they were in position beside the fieldstones that made up the fireplace. She held the figurine out to Angelica.

"It has a hole in the bottom shaped like a celtic cross," said Angelica.

"And see here beside the fireplace?" asked Lisa, pointing. "There is a double line of crosses carved in the wood all around the stones of the fireplace. Each has been hand carved, so they are all different. The second one over and seventh one down on the right side of the fireplace is a perfect fit for the figurine key." She placed the bottom of the figurine over the carved cross beside the fireplace. It fit inside the hollow at the base of the little horse perfectly. "Then you turn it in a complete circle, like this," said Lisa, turning the figurine.

There was a small click, and Lisa pulled the figurine away. The cross looked just as it had before, but this time a sliver of light glowed beside it. Lisa put her fingers into the

crack and pulled. Angelica gasped when a door opened in the wall in front of them. Bright light spilled out into the sitting room.

"Mr. Pickering must have left the light on last time he was in here," said Lisa. "Come on, let's get inside and shut the door. I don't feel safe out here." She stepped inside the tiny room and, when Angelica followed her, Lisa grabbed the handle on the inside of the door and closed it. The door clicked shut, locking from the inside.

"The only way to open it from the outside is with the key, right?" asked Angelica.

"Yes, and we have it with us," Lisa said, holding the figurine up for Angelica to see. "And we can look into the sitting room if we want, but first let's turn the light off or it will shine out the peephole." She put the figurine down on a desk next to the wall and then switched off the light. In the blackness, Lisa reached for the wood covering the peephole and slid it aside.

A pinpoint of pale light opened on the wall and Angelica bent to look out the peephole. "I wonder if we should have turned off the lamp in the sitting room before we came in here," she said.

"It won't take long to search the Priest's Hole," Lisa said beside her. She snapped on the light again and closed the peephole. "It's not very big."

Angelica turned to investigate. Lisa was right. The Priest's Hole was narrow, though it was quite long. She realized it must stretch the entire length from the fireplace to the outside wall of the sitting room. A desk sat beside them at the fireplace end of the Priest's Hole and, at the other end, Angelica could see a landing. Her eyes followed the underside of the stairs as the stairway rose steeply from the landing, arching over their heads. Bookshelves, cupboards, and an old-fashioned sink lined the length of the Priest's Hole. "We can start with the desk," suggested Angelica. "Then if we do not find it, we can search everything else as we move toward the stairs."

"Good plan," said Lisa and pulled out one of the drawers.

"I hope there are no more secret compartments or rooms to find," added Angelica. "It would be nice if everything was obvious for once."

"Well it looks like you get your wish," Lisa said and held up a sealed envelope. "It has my name written on it."

I know they came into the house, but where did they go? Hey, what's that? Voices! They are here, close. Very close. They're in the sitting room. Did I leave that light on? Or did they?

Voices again, too quiet to understand. And they're coming from behind the wall! A secret room! Finally it makes sense. No wonder I couldn't find it. Now all I need to do is wait for them. I'll turn out the lamp so they can't see me and then I'll grab them when they come out. Even if there's another exit to the hidden room, they'll have to walk right past the sitting room door. Every other exit out of the house is blocked: one of the things I had to do to keep my uncle in. Looks like it will come in handy one more time.

But still I need to be careful. That kid is too smart and quick for her own good. It'll be easier to catch her if I can get as close as I can before I grab her.

"What is in it?" asked Angelica, her amber eyes flashing.

Lisa held the envelope tight against her chest for a moment. *This is what Mr. Pickering died for,* she thought. *Whatever is in here, Jimmy wanted it bad enough to murder his uncle.* Slowly she opened the envelope and slid out the stapled papers. Angelica looked over her shoulder as she began to read. "It's his will," said Lisa quietly. "It's Mr. Pickering's will."

"But why would it be addressed to you?" asked Angelica, skimming down the page. Suddenly she gasped.

"What is it?" said Lisa, who had still only read the first few sentences. Most of the words were long and difficult and she didn't know what they meant.

"Let me finish reading it to make sure it says what I think it says," said Angelica. "Then I will tell you."

Lisa handed her the will and Angelica turned the page and continued to read. She read the next page and then the next. Finally she lowered the will. "You are not going to believe this, Lisa," she said quietly. "But he left everything to you."

"What?" said Lisa a little louder than she intended.

"He not only left Evergreen Manor to you, but all his money and the horses and his car and…well, everything," said Angelica.

"But I thought he would leave everything to Jimmy," said Lisa. "Jimmy is his family. I don't understand."

110

"Maybe he did leave it to Jimmy at first," said Angelica, looking back at the top page. "This will is dated just two weeks ago. He could have changed it when he realized what kind of person Jimmy really is."

Lisa pulled out the chair at the desk and sat down. "And somehow Jimmy knew he had changed it. Maybe Mr. Pickering even told him, hoping Jimmy would become a better person," she whispered. "But instead of changing, Jimmy decided to murder his uncle. He knew he had to find the new will and destroy it before anyone read it, or he wouldn't inherit anything." A stony look crept over Lisa's face. "I am so angry!" she said, her voice as hard as nails. "At Jimmy and at myself too. I should have figured it out. I am so stupid! Why didn't I see what was happening? All that time I was just glad that Jimmy was here, thinking my dad was the dangerous one."

"Lisa, like I have told you, it is not your fault," said Angelica. "Do not blame yourself because you did not understand the actions of an evil person. Mr. Pickering would not blame you and neither would your dad. And neither do I."

"But I blame myself," said Lisa. "I was the only one who could've known. The only one who had a chance to save him."

"But you did not have a chance to figure it out," said Angelica insistently. "That is my point. Jimmy made sure you were not over here during the day. He knew if you saw Mr. Pickering there was a chance he could signal to you for help. When you had to sneak over in the middle of the night, there was no way you could see what was happening."

"I saw them in the library last night," confessed Lisa. "I saw Jimmy searching the books. When Mr. Pickering came into the room, he looked so sick and weak but still I just turned away to go take care of the horses. I didn't stay to see what would happen." A sob caught in her throat.

"Lisa, listen to me," said Angelica firmly. "Jimmy is the one to blame. He is the only one at fault. You had nothing to do with Mr. Pickering's murder!" Lisa looked down at her hands. She was silent for a full minute before Angelica spoke again. "You must believe me, Lisa," said Angelica. "You must let go of the guilt. There was nothing you could do to stop Jimmy's crime. But there is something you can do now. We can make sure he pays for what he did to Mr. Pickering. We can make sure the will comes to light."

"We have to give it to someone as soon as we can," said Lisa, looking up. "I couldn't bear to have Jimmy live at Evergreen Manor, especially now. And what would happen to the horses if he ever became their owner? It's just too horrible to think about."

"Then we have to take the will back to your house, wake up your mom and dad and tell them everything that has happened," said Angelica. "They can call the police."

"My dad will be so angry at me when he finds out I've been sneaking around," said Lisa. She stood and reached for the will. "But, you're right. I'm going to tell them everything." She slipped the will back into the envelope, then folded the envelope in half and shoved it in her jacket pocket. Then she turned to go.

"Wait," said Angelica as Lisa reached for the doorknob. "We need to make sure it is safe to leave. I can feel Jimmy is near, but I cannot tell where he is." She turned off the light and reached out in the darkness, feeling for the cover of the peephole. Lisa heard a slight scrape as Angelica pushed the cover aside. When Angelica breathed in sharply, she felt a prickle of fear begin at the back of her neck.

"What is it?" she whispered. She heard Angelica close

the peephole and then fumble for the light switch. When light filled the small space, Lisa could see that Angelica's face had grown paler.

"The light is out," Angelica whispered. "Someone turned off the sitting room lamp. Jimmy must be out there. Waiting for us."

"What are we going to do?" asked Lisa, then clamped her mouth shut, immediately angry at the fear that had crept into her tone. With an effort, she controlled her voice and spoke again. "Maybe he was listening at the wall and knows we've found the will."

"We could go out the other exit," said Angelica, dropping her voice to a faint whisper. "But if he is listening in the sitting room, he would know when we stopped talking and then go looking for us."

"If he's even in the sitting room still. Maybe he's looking for us right now," whispered Lisa. "You couldn't see him?"

"It is too dark," said Angelica. "But it makes sense that he is still there. Why else would he turn the light out? He must be hiding in the dark, waiting for us."

"If he can hear us talking in here, how are we going to get him to stay in the sitting room while we escape through the upstairs exit?" asked Lisa.

"You stay here and talk, pretending to be both of us having a conversation and I will go get help," suggested Angelica quietly.

"Good idea," said Lisa. "But I should go, not you. I know my way around the house and I know the way to the back door. You just keep Jimmy here in the sitting room."

"But what if I am wrong, Lisa?" whispered Angelica. "What if he is walking around the house looking for us?"

"We're going to have to take that chance," whispered Lisa. "But I think you're right. I think he's waiting for us in

114

the sitting room, thinking we're going to bring the will right to him."

"Good luck," said Angelica, her eyes worried. "Please be careful, Lisa. I wish I could tell you exactly where he is but I cannot. All I can tell you is that he is there, somewhere. If he finds you, call me. I will come as fast as I can. But call loudly. I do not know if I will hear you otherwise."

"I'll be careful, and good luck to you too," Lisa whispered. Quickly she moved toward the back of the Priest's Hole. When she started to climb the stairs, she heard Angelica begin to talk. She spoke in a normal voice, then, in a slightly different tone, answered herself. The faked conversation became quiet as Lisa moved steadily up the stairs.

The steps were high and steep, climbing up two stories in a short distance. As Lisa climbed higher, she found that the light didn't penetrate the gloom around the top stairs. She felt her way up the last few steps with her hands. Finally she felt the rough door in front of her. She reached up and found the doorknob. It was cool in her hand.

Down below she could still hear the murmur of Angelica's faked conversation. It sounded so safe and comforting, and Lisa had to fight with herself to not hurry back down the stairs. *I wish we could just wait for Jimmy to leave,* thought Lisa. *But no. I have to do this. It's the only thing I can do to help make up for my stupidity. I'm the one who has to go, because I'm the one that messed up and let Mr. Pickering die. Not Angelica.*

With that thought, Lisa turned the doorknob in her hand. There was a quiet click and she pushed the door open a crack. She put her eye to the opening and searched what she could see of the room. The master bedroom looked deserted. Quietly Lisa stepped out into the room and closed the door to the Priest's Hole behind her.

Like a lithe shadow, she slipped to the bedroom door. The door hung ajar and without touching it, Lisa looked through the crack. The upstairs hall seemed to be deserted as well. The moonlight spilled from the window at the end of the hallway, trickling across the floor toward the giant staircase that led to the story below.

The third floor hallway had always been one of Lisa's favorite places in her old home. The window overlooked the stable and the pastures beyond, and the window seat provided a perfect place to read. Paintings lined the walls of the wide hallway and she liked them all, but the one beside the window seat had always been extra special to her. The portrait was of an 8 or 9-year-old girl holding a lamb in her lap. The girl's face, bent to look into the lamb's eyes, had always given Lisa a feeling of peace.

But the hallway had changed. All the paintings still hung in the right places. The window seat looked the same. *But everything feels wrong*, thought Lisa. She noticed that the giant potted fig tree beside the window seat was dead. It's bony spines sliced through the moonlight like fleshless fingers. Lisa shuddered and looked toward the stairs.

Slowly she crept into the hallway and slid along the wall until she was at the top of the staircase. The banister curved gracefully downward into the darkness. Lisa felt the back of her neck tingle in fear when she realized she couldn't see the bottom of the stairs. *He could be waiting for me down there,* she realized. *And there is no other way down but by these stairs. I've got to pray that he's waiting for us in the sitting room, thinking there is only one exit to the Priest's Hole.*

Lisa crept down the stairs, one by one. She walked near the banister and tested each step with her foot to be sure the stairs wouldn't squeak. She hoped with each step to see into

116

the gloom at the bottom of the staircase. The moonlit hall behind her was a lighted backdrop, and Lisa knew she would stand out like a dark moving form against the soft light. She could imagine Jimmy standing in the shadows at the bottom of the stairs, waiting to leap out at her. Her legs ached to run, to thunder down the stairs and then race for the back door. Her mind could barely stand the suspense of some possibly watching her, waiting for her.

But if Jimmy is in the sitting room, he would hear me for sure if I ran, Lisa reminded herself. *I must stay calm. He's probably waiting inside and there is no need for him to come out as long as he hears Angelica speaking, and I am completely and totally quiet.*

When she reached the second floor, Lisa paused at the head of the next flight of stairs. She was in darkness now. The moonlight from the third floor didn't spread to the second. She peered into the shadows as her eyes adjusted to the darkness. The entrance hall below looked deserted, but it was too dark to tell for sure.

Now comes the hardest part of all, she thought. *I can't make a single sound. I can't even scuff my shoes against the stairs.* She clung to the banister and tested each step as she slowly, slowly descended.

Just three stairs away from the bottom of the staircase, Lisa thought she heard something. Something like breath being exhaled. Terror shot through her and she froze on the steps, her heart thudding wildly. Her ears searched for another noise, but there was nothing. It was dead quiet. *But I know I heard something,* Lisa thought, terrified. *He's just inside the sitting room door and he's waiting for me. He just doesn't know I heard him. He doesn't know I know he's there yet, and he's waiting for me to come closer.* Two seconds ticked by like hours and suddenly Lisa knew what to do.

117

With an explosion of movement, she leaped from the stairs and landed in the entrance hall. Then she raced toward the front door. She grabbed the doorknob and pulled with all her strength. The door opened an inch, then banged shut. The chain was on! She turned to run back the way she had come, but he was there, a black form between her and freedom.

"And where do you think you're going?" he quietly drawled in his thin voice.

Instantly, Lisa felt her fear disappear and, in its place, rage awakened again. "You murderer!" she spit at him, her voice low but deadly serious. "You killed him. You killed Mr. Pickering."

His only reply was a laugh. Lisa couldn't control herself anymore. With a growl of rage, she ran toward him. Jimmy mustn't have seen her in the dark because he was unprepared for Lisa's head hitting him in the stomach. With an "oof," he staggered backward and fell with Lisa on top of him. Before he could grab her she rolled away, sprung to her feet and ran toward the corridor that led to the back door.

When she reached the corridor, Lisa slowed to a walk. The corridor was dark and she didn't want to risk turning the light on, just in case Jimmy thought she was going to run and hide instead. Her heart pounded like crazy and she held her hand over her mouth as she moved, to make her breath as silent as possible. Quickly and quietly, she moved toward the door. But when she reached the end of the short corridor, it was not the door she felt beneath her fingers. It was a heavy oak chest, butted up against the door.

Suddenly light flooded the enclosed space. Lisa's hand instinctively went to her eyes, shielding them from the overhead light bulb. Jimmy was standing at the end of the corridor, his hand on the light switch.

"Good thing I had to block all the exits to make sure my dear uncle would stay where he was supposed to," he said and smiled coldly. Then he began to walk toward Lisa. "Now we get to have some fun too."

As soon as he was close enough, Lisa kicked hard at his shins and, though Jimmy recoiled in pain for a moment, she wasn't able to run past him. The smile was gone from his face when he came at her the second time. He grabbed her by her hair and pulled her head back. The pain made tears spring into Lisa's eyes. She could feel him search her pockets and pull the folded envelope holding the will from her jacket. Then he pushed her away from him. Lisa hit the oak chest hard and slid to the floor. She bit her lip and breathed sharply as she waited for the pain to subside.

Jimmy stood in front of her, reading the will. After a minute, he looked up. "So close and yet so far," he sneered. "I bet you were glad he was dead when you read this."

"You make me sick," Lisa said, feeling her anger return as the pain diminished. "I can't believe you were related to him. He was the nicest man I ever knew, and you killed him."

Jimmy shoved the will back into its envelope, his fingers twitching, then he slipped it into his left jacket pocket. His hand shot out, and he grabbed Lisa by the hair again and jerked her to her feet. "You think you're better than me? You think you are any different? I know you were glad he was dead when you read the will."

"You're wrong. I wasn't glad. Don't you see that all this is just stuff?" said Lisa. "It's not important. Mr. Pickering was important. He mattered. His stuff didn't matter at all."

"Well," said Jimmy as he began to drag her back toward the front door. "I'm glad you feel that way because this 'stuff' will never belong to you and, what's more, you'll be happy to know you'll be seeing my uncle again real soon."

"What…what do you mean?" said Lisa, her anger fading quickly in the renewed face of her fear.

They had reached the entrance hall. "Exactly what you think I mean," said Jimmy as he dragged her to the front door. He began to fumble with the chain high on the door. "I'm going to make it look like an accident and, at the same time, I'll cover up the evidence of my uncle's murder."

As she listened to the chain rattling in its groove, Lisa realized what Jimmy meant. *He's planning to kill me,* she thought. A strange lethargy started to float over her, making the chain sound a million miles away. Lisa fought against it but she felt she was slowly sinking into shock. *As if my brain won't accept this is real,* she realized. *But I've got to do something.* She thought of her mom and Molly and how sad they would be if she died. She could picture them crying in each other's arms. She thought of Jupiter and how he wouldn't understand where she had gone. But it was when she thought of her dad that she felt her fighting spirit return. *He doesn't need any more sadness or anger,* she thought. *He needs me to stay strong.*

With a great lunge, she threw herself backward, then cried out in pain. It felt as if every hair on her head was being pulled out by the roots. "Angelica!" she shrieked. "Help!"

Lisa didn't see Jimmy's fist fly toward her, but when it struck her high on the cheekbone, her head snapped back and she cried out in despair and anguish. Then everything went dark. She wasn't even aware of falling to the floor.

That cry! It echoed through the Priest's Hole like a restless spirit. I must go to Lisa.

Jimmy. He has her. Oh poor Lisa, crumpled there on the floor. And the look in his eyes is so full of hatred. How can I stop him when I am not allowed to force him to do anything? I am sure he will not listen to my words. He has gone too far to back down now. Somehow I must trick him into letting her go. If I can make him believe I could force him, if I scare him, then maybe he will leave her. I will do the Glowing.

There's the other one, the beautiful one. Good thing I knocked out the kid. Two of them might have been too much to handle if they'd attacked together. But little Lisa isn't going to be doing much for a few minutes.

Good! The door is unlocked. Now I'll just grab the blonde and take them both to the stable.

First there was a feeling of just *being*. Lisa felt so peaceful and calm that she didn't want to open her eyes. But then she became aware of the pain. Her cheekbone felt as if it had exploded. Lisa reached up and touched the skin of her face. It was swelling already. *What happened?* she wondered. Then she remembered. Jimmy had hit her. He was planning to kill her. Just like he killed Mr. Pickering. Her eyes sprung open and she tried to rise.

Jimmy was standing with his back to her. Lisa staggered to her feet behind him, leaning on the door with her head down. A wave of dizziness washed over her and she almost fell.

She could hear Angelica's voice, clear as a bell, and looked up. Angelica was standing in front of Jimmy commanding him to let Lisa go, her voice strong. Lisa watched as Jimmy walked toward Angelica, his hands clenched into fists.

"Run Angelica," cried Lisa, weakly. "Get help! Get my dad!"

But Angelica stepped toward Jimmy. Her powerful voice rang out again, commanding Jimmy to let Lisa go and to give himself up to the police. Jimmy laughed as he reached for her wrist.

Suddenly, sparks burst from Angelica's hands. Lisa gasped as Angelica reached toward Jimmy and he jumped backward. In his haste, he tripped over his own feet and sprawled across the floor, falling toward the front door.

"Who are you?" he croaked. "What are you?"

The sparks were moving up Angelica's arms. When they reached her torso, they spread quickly around her entire body to an intense glowing. Her hair swirled around her and light glistened like stars over the spun gold. Her eyes glowed like molten lava. "Who I am does not matter." Angelica's voice seemed to boom from all around her. Lisa wasn't even sure that her lips had moved. "What matters is who you are. You are a murderer, and you will be stopped!"

Lisa realized this was her chance to escape a little too late. As Jimmy slid backward toward the door, pulling himself with his arms, Lisa staggered to the side. But Jimmy noticed her movement. His hand flashed out like a striking snake and fastened around her ankle. As Lisa tried to pull away, he looked at Angelica, watching her closely with narrowed eyes.

Instinctively, Lisa reached down and began to claw at his hand. In a flash, his hand left her ankle and fastened around her wrist. He didn't seem to notice her struggles as he climbed to his feet. "So why haven't you stopped me yet?" he asked Angelica in a cold, calculating voice.

Angelica stepped forward, light streaming from every pore in her body. "Let her go!" Even Angelica's voice seemed to be filled with light, and Lisa closed her eyes against the brightness. There was silence for a long moment as Angelica and Jimmy faced each other.

Then Jimmy jerked Lisa back toward the door. "I don't think you will stop me, witch," he spat out. "I don't think you can. If you could have done it, you'd have done it by now." He stepped backward again, pulling Lisa with him.

With horror, Lisa saw Angelica's light fade just a tiny bit. *He's right,* she realized. *Angelica can't stop him. She has some strange powers, but she can't stop him. And now he*

125

knows that. Now he's going to kill me and then maybe her too.

"I was right. You can't do anything," Jimmy sneered at Angelica. "Now I know what you are. You're just a freak."

"No," whispered Lisa, more to herself than Jimmy. "She's an angel. Molly knew." She felt Jimmy's grip tighten on her wrist even more, though she didn't know how it could be possible. Her fingers already tingled from lack of circulation.

Suddenly Jimmy turned his back to Angelica and stalked out the door, pulling Lisa along with him. She jerked backward with all her strength but he only laughed as he walked into the night. Lisa looked back at Angelica with pleading eyes and saw her slump to the ground. Angelica's glowing was fading rapidly and the dying light seemed to be taking all her strength with it. Then Jimmy jerked Lisa toward the front paddock.

"Go get my dad," Lisa yelled. *Even though it will be too late by then,* she suddenly realized. *Jimmy will have already murdered me, and my dad will think it was an accident. Even if Angelica tells them otherwise, would they believe her? She isn't really even human.*

"We're going to get rid of that horse of yours at the same time," Jimmy muttered to Lisa. "Call him to come here."

"No," Lisa said firmly.

Jimmy's hand came down across her face again, and Lisa cried out and fell to the ground. "Call him!" he yelled.

"No!" Lisa yelled back just as loud. She put her free arm over her head when she noticed Jimmy's hand rise to strike her.

When she heard Jimmy laugh, Lisa cautiously lowered her arm. He was looking into the pasture. Then Lisa heard Jupiter's hoofbeats on the grass, trotting toward her. "No Jupie," she yelled. "Go back." She ducked as Jimmy's hand made a swipe at her. "Run, Jupie," she shouted once more and then she was pulled to her feet and Jimmy's hand was over her mouth.

"Now listen good, you little brat," he whispered. Lisa cringed as his hot breath touched her face. "Either you bring him into the stable or I'll shoot him right here, right in front of you. You understand?" He held Lisa still for a moment then slowly took his hand off her mouth. Lisa turned to see Jupiter walk toward her in the moonlight, the silky radiance flowing over his black coat like water. Topper was right behind him, looking like a fluid silver sculpture. *Can I take the chance that Jimmy is lying to me?* she thought desperately. *How can I know if he really has a gun?*

Jupiter reached the fence. His ears were pinned back against his head and he glared at Jimmy, then his head snaked over the top rail. His teeth snapped together just inches from Jimmy's face. Jimmy leaped back, holding Lisa in front so she was between him and Jupiter.

Suddenly he pushed her forward. Lisa fell against the fence, then spun around. Jimmy was standing with his hand in his jacket pocket. He was holding something, something that looked almost too big for his pocket. After a moment, Lisa realized it must be his gun. "Get his halter," Jimmy demanded and shoved the gun harder against the material.

With hesitant steps, Lisa moved toward the gate. She could feel the numbness wash over her again. All her strength seemed to be evaporating into fear that was too strong to fight. She reached for Jupiter's halter with shaking hands and called him toward her.

After Jupiter was haltered, Jimmy told her to lead the gelding to the stable. With numb muscles, Lisa opened the gate and led Jupiter out. She didn't think to shut the gate behind him and could hear Topper's hoofbeats following them as they walked toward the stable. Topper followed them halfway, then suddenly turned and galloped back toward the house. The relief of at least one of them being safe struck into the core of Lisa's fear and unexpectedly she found her courage. She thought of leaping onto Jupiter's back and racing away. But she felt so weak still. So exhausted. How could she pull herself up in time when Jimmy was standing right behind them holding a gun?

He's going to kill us anyway, Lisa reminded herself. *I've got to do something.* Her steps began to slow as she started to plan their escape. *Maybe if I jump up far enough to lie across his back, then Jupiter could carry me away. But he would have to go so slowly. I might fall off unless I'm all the way on his back. Then Jimmy will catch us anyway. If only Jupie wasn't so big. I know he would fight Jimmy if I let him, but I can't let him do that if Jimmy has a gun. And I can't leave Jupie to fight it out alone. But what...*

"We don't have all night," Jimmy snarled at Lisa. "Pick up the pace."

Lisa began to walk a little faster. The stable was almost in front of them now. *I've got to think of something. Anything. And right now,* she thought desperately, but her mind remained blank. The dark form of the stable loomed up in front of her. Jimmy commanded her to stop, then moved around in front of Lisa and Jupiter.

This is my only chance! Lisa realized when she heard Jimmy cursing as he searched for the light switch. Quickly, she grabbed Jupiter's mane and sprung as high as she could. She didn't jump high enough and slid off his side, then gathered herself and desperately leaped again. This time her elbow made it over his backbone and, with her other hand still clutching his mane, she hoisted herself up with her arms, then slid her leg over Jupiter's back.

Suddenly, light burst from the stable. Jimmy's right hand shot back into his pocket just as Lisa straightened on Jupiter's back. He pulled out a silver handgun and pointed it at Jupiter's chest. Lisa froze.

"Get off right now or your horse gets it in the heart," said Jimmy. His voice was as cold as icicles dropping to the ground.

He's going to kill us anyway, Lisa thought again and slowly reached toward the lead rope lying across Jupiter's neck. *All I have to do is turn him and gallop away. There's a chance he'll miss us, though probably not a very good one.* Lisa couldn't take her eyes from the gun, glistening in the light from the stable. It looked so evil. Death was inside of it, Jupiter's death. If she tried to escape. Lisa pulled her hand back and, with tears in her eyes, slid from Jupiter's back.

If I try to escape now, it's like I've done something to kill Jupiter, she thought. *Maybe Jimmy is going to kill us anyway, but I refuse to do anything that might hurt Jupie. I couldn't live with myself if I got away and Jupie didn't. If we get away at all, we're going to do it together!*

How am I going to save Lisa when I cannot even stand? I must save her. That is why I was sent here. But the Glowing took too much life-energy. I have no more to give. Unless...what is that I hear? The door is being pushed open by a soft muzzle. Hoofbeats across the floor.

Topper.

His tears fall one by one like golden kisses raining down on my weariness. And my strength is returning in waves!

We will ride together, Topper and I. And the others will help. We will fall upon the foe like an unexpected tidal wave. A tsunami! He will be crushed!

Reluctantly, Lisa led Jupiter into the stable. Jimmy motioned for her to put the horse into his stall. At first Jupiter hesitated at the stall door. Lisa allowed him to lean forward and sniff the straw where Mr. Pickering had lain. Then when Lisa walked ahead of him into the stall, he followed closely behind her, his muzzle snuffling her hair.

"Come out and shut the door behind you," commanded Jimmy.

Lisa wanted to refuse but the image of the gun flashed into her mind. She glanced at Jimmy. His hands were empty, but there was a bulge in his right jacket pocket.

"Leave the halter on him and get out here," he said when Lisa turned and began to unbuckle the halter from Jupiter's head. "I'm tired of waiting. Let's get this over with."

Lisa unclipped the lead rope from Jupiter's halter as she turned toward Jimmy. She held it behind her back and stepped out of the stall, pushing the door shut behind her. When she heard the latch to the stall click, she whipped the lead rope from around her back and swung the clip end toward Jimmy. He sprang back but not far enough. The metal hit him on the side of the face.

Instantly, Lisa swung at him again but this time he was ready. He grabbed the end of the lead rope and jerked. Lisa went flying toward him. With one swift movement, Jimmy let go of the lead rope and grabbed her hair again.

"You stupid brat!" he screamed, his face red where the

clip had struck him. "You're going to get what you deserve! Right now." He jerked her around so her back was to him. Lisa kicked at him behind her, but her foot missed when he jerked her arms together behind her back. Jupiter struck against the stall door with his front hoof and Lisa wished she hadn't pushed the door shut. Jupiter was furious at Jimmy. She could read it in his eyes and his flattened-back ears. Then she felt the lead rope wind around her wrists. Jimmy was tying her up.

As soon as the rope was tight around her wrists, Jimmy tied the end of the lead rope around her ankles. Then he pushed her. Lisa fell toward Jupiter's stall. In mid-fall she tried to twist her body so that she would land on her shoulder, but there wasn't time. Her head hit the wall beside Jupiter's stall and she bounced onto the floor.

Though her head throbbed in pain, Lisa wiggled to a sitting position. Jimmy was standing over her, his cheek as red as a beet. Lisa turned her head to the side and closed her eyes as he bent to strike her. The blow never fell. Instead she heard laughter—cold, cruel laughter.

Lisa opened her eyes to see Jimmy reach into his right jacket pocket and pull out his cigarettes. He put an unlit one in his mouth, then reached into his pocket and pulled out the gun. He smiled as he slowly pointed it at Lisa's heart.

"Any last words?" he drawled.

Lisa's mind was numb. All she could think of was the gun barrel pointing at her. She wished that at least she had been able to save Jupiter. Or Angelica. She realized Angelica was probably still slumped in the entrance hall of the Manor. *I hope she had enough strength to hide. There's a place under the stairs that Jimmy may not know about.*

"No? Too proud to beg for your own life?" said Jimmy in a quiet voice, but Lisa wasn't fooled into thinking his soft

133

tone meant he was having second thoughts about killing her. "Okay then," said Jimmy and he moved the gun so it was pointing at her head. Lisa watched in horror as his finger tightened on the trigger.

"Pow," whispered Jimmy and Lisa jumped. Then Jimmy moved the gun barrel toward the end of his cigarette. He pulled the trigger and a tiny, quiet flame flickered from the end of the barrel.

When she realized what was happening, Lisa felt an incredible rage swarm over her. The gun was really a lighter! A cigarette lighter! She felt her face grow hot with unexpressed rage. *I could have ridden away,* she realized. *I could have turned Jupie and galloped off and been home in five minutes, and Jimmy couldn't have done a thing to stop me. But instead I gave up!*

"I'll go get your freaky friend as soon as I enjoy my smoke," said Jimmy taunting her. "Then you and her and your precious horses will all go up in flames. Oh yes, and the will too. The will that no one knows about but you and me and the freak back there in the house." He inhaled another lung full of smoke, then took the cigarette from his smirking mouth. "This has been a productive night," he continued. "I thought I would only get to kill the horses and get rid of the evidence, but now I can burn the will and you too." He stopped and inhaled again. "It'll be so sad," he continued with false concern in his voice. "So tragic. They'll think you were upset that your horse was accused of murder and you came over to the stable to steal him away. They'll think you led him into the stable to tack him up and then lit a candle so no one would see the light and know you were here. And then, oh so terrible, the candle fell into the straw and poof! The whole stable went up in flames."

"They won't believe that story. They'll know Jupiter didn't do it," said Lisa, her voice hard with anger. She could hear a quiet buzzing noise, far away. "They did tests on his hooves and the tests will prove he's innocent. They won't believe I would steal him away if I knew he could be proved innocent."

"Oh didn't I tell you?" asked Jimmy with wide eyes. "My new girlfriend, Tiffany, works at the forensics lab. She's going to discover, first thing in the morning, that the samples taken from your horse's hooves have been misplaced. Lost." He inhaled again and when he started to speak, smoke poured from his mouth. "They're so disorganized over there, you know," he said. "And the poor, dear horse isn't going to be around much longer for them to take new samples."

"What about your car rental slip?" asked Lisa, trying to think of anything she could use to stop Jimmy. *He doesn't need to know that the slip is still in my pocket,* she thought. "They'll find it in my room and investigate it. They'll find out that the car was rented to you: Thomas J. Short. The J must be for James or Jimmy."

A flash of doubt crossed Jimmy's face. He inhaled again, drawing deeply on the cigarette, then slowly exhaled. "That's assuming they even find the car rental slip," he replied in a nervous voice. "Your mom will probably just throw it out. She'll be so sad when she boxes up all your stuff that she'll hardly notice it."

"The police will suspect you anyway," predicted Lisa. "They're going to look for your fingerprints and they'll catch you."

"But what's wrong with my fingerprints being here?" asked Jimmy, confident again. "I've been staying with my uncle and taking care of him while he's been ill, just like a good, concerned nephew should."

136

"They'll find out somehow," said Lisa, her voice rising. "I know they will. You can't have thought of everything and the police aren't stupid. They'll catch you."

Suddenly Lisa stopped speaking. The noise she had noticed earlier was quickly growing louder. The sound seemed familiar, like a hive of bees or like the wind in the trees. Like a river. Lisa pushed it to the back of her mind again as she looked up at Jimmy. "They'll ask you where you were," she continued. "What are you going to tell them?"

"Oh, you don't need to worry about me," said Jimmy. "I have an alibi. I was apparently at the opera with Tiffany tonight, and I'll show them the ticket stub to prove it. How can I be here, murdering my uncle, when I'm treating my new girlfriend to a night on the town? And, you forget that in a few minutes there's going to be no one left alive who can even tell them I was here tonight."

The strange noise was becoming too loud to ignore. Even Jimmy stopped speaking and looked up toward the ceiling. When he looked back at Lisa, his face was puzzled. But now Lisa knew what the noise was. She had heard it before and every time she had been with Angelica.

Suddenly, Jupiter's scream pierced the air. He reared in his stall, striking at the stall door with his front hooves. Firefly wheeled around and kicked at the door to her stall and Dakota added his neigh to Jupiter's. Lisa would have covered her ears with her hands if they hadn't been tied behind her back. Instead she began to struggle against her bonds. Jimmy turned toward the horses, stunned. "What the…" he said, then stopped when the door to the stable burst open.

Topper rushed inside with Angelica bent low on his back. Jimmy threw down his glowing cigarette and jumped toward them, reaching for Angelica. The gray gelding reared into the air, his front hooves flashing in Jimmy's face. Firefly's back hooves hit her stall door again and the door went flying halfway across the stable. In a second she was out of her stall. She jumped toward Jimmy with her teeth bared. Angelica raised her hand to Firefly and the mare stopped in her tracks, though she looked murderously at the man standing in front of her. Then they began to circle Jimmy. Lisa heard Jupiter strike at his stall door again, but she didn't look away from the four beings in front of her.

Topper and Firefly stalked around Jimmy with Angelica still riding on Topper's back. Even as Lisa struggled to free her hands from the tight rope, she couldn't help but notice how perfectly Angelica was balanced on the gelding's back. Her hair shone a glistening gray in the stable light, the same color as Topper's sleek side. It spilled over his back like a silver waterfall, blending perfectly into his coat. The sound Lisa had heard was emanating from Angelica like electricity. As the two horses and the girl swarmed around Jimmy, the sound ebbed and flowed.

Jimmy fumbled in his pocket for his gun lighter. A triumphant look flashed onto his face when he pointed it at Angelica, then was instantly replaced with shock as Topper struck out with his front hoof and the lighter went flying across the stable. With a look of horror on his face, Jimmy made a dash for freedom. He dove between Firefly's head and Topper's hindquarters and ran for the door. Firefly was right behind him as he raced into the night and Topper and Angelica spun around to follow him.

Then Lisa noticed the flame. So tiny. So deadly. Just a foot away from her in the straw. "Angelica!" she shrieked. "His cigarette started a fire!"

Angelica turned her head and brought Topper to a sliding stop. She leaped from his back and then stood on tiptoes and

138

whispered a quick message into his ear. Topper sprung forward and disappeared through the door as Angelica raced toward the flames.

"A saddle blanket," yelled Lisa, frantically struggling against her bonds. "Get a saddle blanket and smother the fire." She rolled a few feet away from the quickly spreading blaze as Angelica disappeared into the tack room. But the fire was spreading too quickly. It raced toward Jupiter's stall and started to climb the wall. Jupiter screamed in panic, bringing Angelica running with the blanket in her hand. She beat at the flames close to the stall door, forcing them to retreat just enough for her to reach out, grab the latch and pull the door open.

But Jupiter wouldn't leave his stall. The flames were all around the door and he was too frightened to run through them. Angelica stepped through the circle of fire and whispered in Jupiter's ear, but he didn't seem to hear her. Instead he stared at the growing flames with wild, rolling eyes. One iron hoof kicked out and hit the back wall of his stall.

"Jupie, come here," called Lisa when she realized that Angelica alone couldn't save the black gelding. "Come to me. I need you." She kicked at the straw as the fire jumped right in front of her. "Jupie," she called again, her voice more desperate.

The black gelding hesitated one more second, then lunged forward. He brushed past Angelica and leaped from the stall, then stood shuddering beside Lisa. In a second, Angelica was beside Lisa as well, fumbling with the knots that tied her hands and feet. Jupiter's stall was filled with flame now and the fire had engulfed the tack room. Lisa began to cough in the black smoke as she tried to breath. The smoke was beginning to make her feel dizzy and sick.

As soon as the rope fell away, Angelica pulled Lisa to her

feet, then boosted her onto Jupiter's back. "Go," she yelled. "Take him to safety."

"But Dakota," protested Lisa between coughing spasms.

"I will get him," said Angelica. "You take Jupiter." She reached up and smacked Jupiter on the hindquarters and he leaped forward as if stung. Lisa kept low to his neck as he trotted toward the door. Just before she passed through the doorway, she saw the brightness of new flame shoot out through the smoke surrounding the hay pile. There was no hope for the stable now. The fire was in the haystack. Then she and Jupiter were outside, surrounded by the blessed cool air.

A few feet from the stable, Lisa asked Jupiter to stop and turn around. Flames were shooting from the doorway they had just left. She vaulted from Jupiter's back and raced toward the stable, hardly noticing when Jupiter turned away from the fire and hurried off into the night. Lisa drew as close to the stable as she could. The heat was almost unbearable. Anxiously, she watched the doorway, searching for Angelica and Dakota's forms against the bright seething flame.

How can they get through that wall of fire? thought Lisa. *How are they going to escape with only the one exit?* Suddenly the flames blew outward as if a monstrous wind was behind them. The hot blast swept past Lisa and she threw her hands over her face to protect herself. After a moment, she peeked between her fingers and looked at the doorway with narrowed eyes, just in time to see Dakota burst from the opening in the flames with his head low and his ears pinned. Angelica was crouched on his back, her face buried in his short mane. Her hair was like a mantle over her and Dakota, a shimmering white with gray and black spots dancing across it.

When Dakota drew alongside Lisa, Angelica sat up straight on the pony's back. "Climb on up," she said as Dakota stopped beside Lisa. "We have to save Jimmy."

"What?" said Lisa, too surprised to move. "Save Jimmy?"

Angelica offered her hand. "I am afraid they will hurt him," she said. "They are so angry." She held out her hand to Lisa and helped Lisa swing onto Dakota's back behind her. Then she urged Dakota into a canter. Quickly they covered the ground between the stable and the house. Dakota seemed to know where to go. His ears were pointing into the darkness. They could hear Jimmy yelling for help, his voice growing louder the nearer they came.

When the rounded the far side of the Manor, Lisa saw the dark form of Jimmy's rental car hidden in the shadows. One of the horses was standing close to the driver's side, broadside to the car. It was Jupiter, squeezing Jimmy up next to his car, holding him in place. Firefly was standing on the other side of Jupiter, reaching over his back and biting at Jimmy as Topper looked on.

Angelica called out to them and Firefly stopped her attack. As soon as Dakota stopped, Lisa slipped from his back and Angelica followed her. Then Angelica motioned to Firefly to turn her hindquarters to Jimmy and back up to him. When Firefly was in place, Angelica signalled Jupiter to step away. Firefly raised one of her back hooves in warning. "Hold still," Angelica commanded Jimmy. "Or Firefly will make short work of you."

Jimmy's eye's glowed with hatred as he glared at Angelica and Lisa, but he held still. Firefly humped her back and pretended she was going to kick him and he cried out, cowering against the car.

"Now hold out the will," said Angelica in a firm voice.

"Hold it toward us." When Jimmy had pulled the will from his pocket, she patted Dakota on the neck. "Go get it, boy," she whispered. Dakota stepped forward confidently. He laid his ears back at Jimmy and reached out with his teeth to grab the will. Then he stepped back to Angelica and Lisa.

The sound of fire truck sirens cut through the air, racing closer and closer. Angelica pressed the will into Lisa's hand. "I must go before they get here," she said urgently. "Do not tell them about me. They will not believe you. Just tell them that you and the horses caught Jimmy. Tell them about Jimmy confessing to murdering Mr. Pickering and how he tried to kill you because of the will."

"But where are you going?" asked Lisa, her eyes round.

"I cannot say. There is not enough time." She stopped when the fire engines turned into the driveway. "I will come back later. There is one more thing left to do."

Lisa turned away to look at the fire engines racing in the driveway, then she turned back to Angelica. "What's left to do?" she asked, but her voice faded away when she saw that Angelica was gone. Lisa clutched the will in her hand and took a deep breath, then looked toward Jimmy with narrowed eyes. He was still cowering against the car. Seeing that he was too afraid of Firefly to move, she turned back toward the approaching fire engines and, walking to the edge of the house, began to wave her arms.

Seconds after the firemen arrived and ran to control the fire, the police pulled into the driveway. Within minutes, Jimmy was arrested and put into the backseat of one of the squad cars. With no door handles and strong-iron mesh between the back seat of the car and the front, it was like a small jail. When Lisa saw him sitting with his head in his hands, she almost felt sorry for him. But then she remembered Mr. Pickering's bruised and broken body, and backed away from the car. As the police car started to pull away, Jimmy looked up. His eyes locked onto Lisa's and she took another step back as his hatred seemed to leap toward her. Then he was gone.

Lisa turned back to the horses. "Come on guys," she said to the four of them, still standing beside Jimmy's rental car. She took Jupiter's halter in her hand and began to lead him toward the back of the house. Obediently, the other three followed.

"Life goes on, and I'm glad it does," she whispered to no one in particular when the smell of the roses in the garden behind the house drifted toward her. "But I am going to miss Mr. Pickering so much." She reached up to stroke Jupiter's neck as they walked.

When they reached the gate to the large back paddock, Lisa swung it open. "You guys will like it in here. It's the farthest from the fire and it has the biggest turnout shelter. I'll come and visit you before I leave tonight, okay?" Jupiter stepped inside the pasture and, one by one, the others followed. Lisa swung the gate shut and latched it behind them, then walked toward the blaze.

She stopped when she turned the corner. The firefighters were black silhouettes moving quickly against the flames. Only three people stood still: a man, a woman and a young girl. With a jolt, Lisa recognized her family with their backs turned to her, their arms around each other. Molly had buried her face in her hands and Lisa could see her mom's shoulder's shaking. *They're afraid I was in the fire,* she realized. *And I would have been, if Angelica hadn't saved us.* Gripping the will in her hand, she hurried toward them, then reached out and touched her dad's arm. He jumped and spun around.

"Lisa!" he said, his voice overflowing with relief. "We were so afraid you..." He stopped speaking and pulled her into his arms. Lisa could feel her mom hug her from behind and Molly latch onto her leg. Their bodies felt so warm and comforting. She hugged her dad back hard and then pulled away. "The firemen and police knew I was okay," she said.

"We just got here," said Lisa's mom. "No one has had time to talk to us yet."

"We were afraid something had happened to you when we discovered you weren't in your room," said her dad. "And then when we saw the light from the fire..." Again he stopped in mid-sentence, but Lisa understood. She knew that some things were far too hard to say.

Molly piped up. "What about D'kota, Lisa? Is he okay?"

Lisa held out her hand. "Come and see," she said. Molly took her hand and Lisa led her toward the back of the house. Her mom and dad followed, relief and thankfulness clearly written on their faces. When Lisa looked back, she smiled to see them walking with their arms around each other. She

145

hadn't seen her mom and dad walk together like that since they had left the Manor. Her hand went to her jacket pocket to feel the will. The Manor was theirs again. It was Mr. Pickering's last gift to her. Lisa felt tears come to her eyes. *I would rather have Mr. Pickering back,* she thought. *He was worth more than all the money in the world.*

When they reached the gate, Lisa called for Jupiter. The family was silent as the horses galloped toward them. Their coats glistened in the moonlight as they pushed up next to the gate.

"D'kota," yelled Molly and reached through the rails. Dakota lowered his pony head and nickered to Molly.

While Molly petted Dakota, Lisa turned to her parents. "Mom? Dad?" she said. "There's a lot of stuff you don't know. A lot of stuff I have to tell you."

It took almost half an hour to tell her parents about everything except Angelica, between all the questions and exclamations of surprise and worry. Finally, Lisa pulled the will out of her pocket. "This is what Mr. Pickering died for," she whispered. "His last gift to me. I wish you could have known what a wonderful person he was."

"I do too," said Lisa's dad. "Can you forgive me for being so angry, Lisa?"

Lisa looked up at him with dark eyes. "I heard you say you would get the Manor back even if you had to kill Mr. Pickering to get it," she said quietly.

Lisa's dad knelt beside her and looked at her with eyes full of sorrow. "Oh Lisa, I am so sorry I said that," he said with a shaking voice. "I hope you realize I wasn't really mad at Mr. Pickering. I would have never hurt him. Please believe me. I was mad at myself and now I'm even angrier that I let my pride stop me from getting to know Mr. Pickering. But this time I know the best way to deal with

146

that anger is to channel it into something positive. I'm really sorry, Lisa, and I promise you I will be a better dad and a better person from now on."

Lisa leaned forward and put her arms around her dad's neck. "It's okay, Daddy," she whispered. Then she added, "And Mr. Pickering would have forgiven you too."

The weeks that followed went by in a blur. There were statements taken by the police and Jimmy was charged with murder, attempted murder, arson, and a number of lesser crimes. Lisa gave them the car rental slip and, after the police officer reprimanded her for not giving it to them right away, he told her that he thought she was very brave. Throughout the questioning, Lisa didn't breathe a word of Angelica's existence and, when she overheard two police officers talking about Jimmy's story of a supernatural being at the house, she listened carefully. The officers seemed to think that Jimmy would be sent to a mental hospital instead of to a jail, but either way, they agreed he would be locked away for the rest of his life.

The family began to make plans for moving back into the Manor, but the paperwork seemed to take forever. Lisa still went over to the Manor everyday to care for the horses. Sometimes her mom and Molly would go with her, and sometimes her dad went along but, once in a while, Lisa was able to get away on her own. Every time she went to visit the horses alone, she hoped to see Angelica there, but weeks passed without a sign of her friend.

Finally the day came for Lisa and her family to move back into their home. Construction on the new stable was well underway and, along with the rest of her family, Lisa was very glad to be back in the house she had grown up in. She put her furniture back in the same places in her room and tried to make it look like it had before she left. The only thing different was a framed picture of Mr. Pickering, standing between Jupiter and Topper, that Lisa had taken on the day of their picnic. She placed the photo on her dresser beside another she had of Jupiter and one of herself with Molly and her mom and dad.

On the day that the new stable was finished, Lisa and her family had a celebration and invited a few friends. They shared carrot cake with the horses in the aisle outside of the stalls as Lisa's dad pointed out that the stable was built to exactly the same specifications as the old stable, except it had some new and updated features. The most important was a sprinkler system in case the stable ever caught fire again, but there was also hot and cold running water in the tack room and one of the extra stalls had been converted to a horse-bathing stall. Everyone was suitable impressed, not only with the stable, but also with the horses who all behaved perfectly.

After everyone had left, the family cleaned up the glasses and plates. While her family carried everything back to the house, Lisa stayed to feed the horses their evening meal. It felt good to be in the stable without all the people there, just the horses quietly munching their grain. *It almost feels like my old stable. It just smells new,* thought Lisa. *And I promise I'm going to appreciate this one while I have it, which hopefully will be for a long, long time.* Slowly and methodically, Lisa groomed all the horses, glorifying in their sleek coats and bright, happy eyes. The stable was so peaceful: the calm after the storm. Finally, Lisa took her grooming kit back to the tack room.

The second she stepped out of the tack room, Lisa could feel a difference in the air. It was an electricity, an energy that hadn't been there before. Then she saw Angelica standing at Firefly's stall. She was whispering in the chestnut mare's ear. Slowly she moved on to Topper's stall and talked to him for a few moments. Lisa waited for her, knowing she was saying farewell to the horses she had grown to love. Finally she moved on to Dakota and then Jupiter. The black gelding nickered when Angelica finished whispering to him and Angelica hugged him around his neck. Then she turned toward Lisa.

"I didn't know if you would be coming," said Lisa softly. "You took so long I had almost given up hope."

"There are many horses in this world that are sad and frightened," answered Angelica with a gentle smile. "I have been far too busy doing what I can to help them."

"Is that what you do?" asked Lisa. "You help horses? Was Molly right? Are you really an angel? A horse angel?"

"Some would call me that, I suppose," said Angelica, shrugging her shoulders. "But really I am just someone who is lucky enough to do good for those I care for. I am just like you. I try to do things to help others."

"You've helped us more than you know. Not just me and the horses, but my family too," said Lisa. "My dad has never been so happy, or my mom and little sister. And my dad has changed. You changed him."

"I did not change him, Lisa." Angelica shook her head as she spoke. "That is one thing you must have seen with Jimmy. I cannot change anyone. People can only change themselves."

"You helped him to see what's important then," said Lisa, smiling.

"I have something for you," said Angelica. She reached her hand to her head and her hair suddenly began to glow and swirl in a wind only available to her. Slowly she reached up into the masses of gold and twined a single hair around

150

her finger. With a sharp tug, the hair came lose and Angelica cupped it inside her hands. "Put out your hand, Lisa," she instructed.

Lisa reached out with an open hand and Angelica dropped the hair into her palm. But it was no longer a hair. It was a necklace, as gold colored as Angelica's locks and as light as down. Lisa took it between two of her fingers and lifted it into the air. The necklace tinkled gently and Lisa could feel soft energy warming her fingers. Speechless, she watched Angelica take it from her, and then Lisa leaned forward so Angelica could slip the necklace around her neck.

"Thank you," she said breathlessly, as she stroked the golden links. "It's the most beautiful necklace I've ever seen."

"It is a magical necklace. And it is part of me," said Angelica. "If you ever need help, just touch it with your finger and call my name. I will come to you then. I can hear the horses if they call to me to help them, but people I cannot hear unless they have the necklace."

"Thank you so much Angelica," said Lisa, tears crowding her voice. She stepped forward and threw her arms around the older girl. Angelica pulled her close for a moment, her arms warm and strong.

Suddenly Lisa felt Angelica stiffen. "Aria," the older girl whispered.

"What?" said Lisa, stepping back.

"Aria is calling me. I can hear her. She is frightened and needs my help," said Angelica, looking at Lisa with her tawny eyes.

"I know you'll save her," said Lisa. "Just like you saved us."

"I will never forget you, Lisa," said Angelica, her voice becoming strangely faint. "You are a brave person. The way you stood up to Jimmy proved that. I admire your strength."

Tears sprung from Lisa's eyes. "Thanks," she whispered and stepped farther back. The horses whinnied farewell as Angelica brightened into a billion particles, her hair flying around her, not as gold, but as light. Then the form of the girl was gone and Angelica became the swirling light. Lisa put her hand over her eyes to protect them from the brightness, but the light even seemed to gleam through her fingers and eyelids.

Then it grew less. Slowly, Lisa lowered her hand and opened her eyes. Angelica was gone. Lisa touched the necklace as she stared at the place Angelica had stood.

"I am strong," she said and smiled.

Aria. I am coming. I can hear your cry on the desert wind, calling for your girl who left you two days ago.

No food.

No water.

Why has she abandoned you in the wilderness?

Do not worry. I will help you. I will protect you and your unborn foal.